W9-BGX-042

WE AWAKEN
CALISTA LYNNE

WITHDRAWN

Harmony Ink

Published by
Harmony Ink Press

5032 Capital Circle SW, Suite 2, PMB# 279, Tallahassee, FL 32305-7886 USA
publisher@harmonyinkpress.com • www.harmonyinkpress.com

This is a work of fiction. Names, characters, places, and incidents either are the product of author imagination or are used fictitiously, and any resemblance to actual persons, living or dead, business establishments, events, or locales is entirely coincidental.

We Awaken
© 2016 Calista Lynne.

Cover Art
© 2016 Aaron Anderson.
aaronbydesign55@gmail.com
Cover content is for illustrative purposes only and any person depicted on the cover is a model.

All rights reserved. This book is licensed to the original purchaser only. Duplication or distribution via any means is illegal and a violation of international copyright law, subject to criminal prosecution and upon conviction, fines, and/or imprisonment. Any eBook format cannot be legally loaned or given to others. No part of this book may be reproduced or transmitted in any form or by any means, electronic or mechanical, including photocopying, recording, or by any information storage and retrieval system, without the written permission of the Publisher, except where permitted by law. To request permission and all other inquiries, contact Harmony Ink Press, 5032 Capital Circle SW, Suite 2, PMB# 279, Tallahassee, FL 32305-7886, USA, or publisher@harmonyinkpress.com.

ISBN: 978-1-63476-995-2
Digital ISBN: 978-1-63476-996-9
Library of Congress Control Number: 2016901422
Published July 2016
v. 1.0

Printed in the United States of America
∞
This paper meets the requirements of
ANSI/NISO Z39.48-1992 (Permanence of Paper).

For Bruce Coville, Roald Dahl, and my parents. You were all there when it started.

Here's to my parents, who are the finest this world has to offer. Thanks for the days in New York and for not judging my openness. A shout-out to Kelsi No, Tiffany Akridge, and Jessica Wyman, who made my words less of a disaster. And whoever is reading this, thank you as well.

ONE

MOTHER SAID there was no change in Reeves at the hospital.

Something must have happened at work for her to come home early enough to visit him, but to find out what would require discussion. I wasn't in the mood to speak with a Magic 8 Ball: shake her up and get nothing but two-word answers. Not that I could blame the woman. When a single day puts your husband in a morgue and your son in a coma, it changes life from being a triple-time waltz to a demo session for hell.

That didn't mean I couldn't resent the emptiness. More family members were lost than those lying on their backs.

She told me about the visit over dinner. I nodded like it was news, then took my leave. The sound of nothing but forks against china was as unbearable as her vacant expression.

I ran down to the basement to stretch; the sting of being a well-practiced ballerina was liberating. When I turned eleven, my dad had installed a large mirror in the basement and a proper floor so I could practice at home instead of having to rely on the studio. It was a safe haven in my own house.

Looking into that mirror now proved even havens were no guarantee of protection.

Earlier that day I visited Dad. His gravestone was starting to lose its reflective sheen and the short, bristly grass no longer shied away from its edges. His soul was whittled down to a few clichéd words, long since memorized, that even he would have laughed at:

Forever in our hearts
Abe James Dinham
Too well loved to ever be forgotten

That was complete crap. Every other headstone in the place bore a similar sentiment yet was left weaponless against the forces of nature, even if they were just the mild New Jersey winters and summers.

Eventually the edges crumble off all our graves.

I wasn't going to say everything else in the world melted away as I danced, but it allowed my thinking to become more mechanical. I stretched on the hardwood floors, now scuffed from hundreds of solo rehearsals, until my thighs burned so fiercely it was impossible to focus on anything other than the sensation.

Impossible to think about the shriveled remains of a greenhouse massacre I found every week on Dad's grave from the blossoms I lined up each visit.

Impossible to think about the driver's license under a year's worth of thrown shoes and forgotten books at the back of my closet. Cars put my father six feet under; I didn't need to add another to the road.

I laced my calloused feet into the stiff pointe shoes and warmed up. Straddle. Splits. Barre work. There wasn't any need to think about them. It all led up to pirouettes, which I lost myself in until the room refused to stop spinning and my inverted toes were suicidal.

Lazy. That's what I was. It was less than two weeks until my auditions with the Manhattan Dance Conservatory, and if I didn't get in, I was screwed. Still, stewing over my fears seemed less painful than actually practicing my choreography. At least Mother had agreed to drive me to the city for the audition. That was one small blessing.

Eventually Mother tapped on the door and told me it was time to go to bed. I didn't dare disagree.

That night, when the lights went out, my brain flashed on as it did so often in the past year. I ended up lying on my mattress watching the fluorescent numbers of the alarm clock, counting them down and focusing on the shapes of the lines turned sideways by my tilted head. I felt like I was floating or on the tipping point of dropping off into slumber.

Generally, when I dreamed, nightmares flickered behind my eyes; whether they sprang from perpetual nervousness or the demise of my family was up for grabs. That night something beautiful swirled through my mind instead. A beach.

Mist hovered over the ground, blocking my view of the sand that was undoubtedly below. This fog was so thick and milky it was as if I was in the middle of a cloud, with cirrus tendrils lapping onto the shore instead of waves. Every sound was subdued under the dove-gray skies and heavy air. Even the splashing waves seemed distant.

I was walking along barefoot, making sure to dig in my toes with each careful step, when a figure appeared in the distance, a small shadow that enlarged as we neared each other. I was soon able to make out the outline of a cloak, flowing around its wearer and fluttering like butterfly wings.

No woman in reality could ever possess such grace. That's how I realized it had to be a dream. Her skin was barely lighter than the dark of night and a hood was pulled so far over her head it was impossible to make out whether she had any hair. The whites of her eyes stood out greatly in contrast to her skin, matching the intense purity of the lace parasol hanging over her right arm. Her clothing was iridescent and looked almost like oil as it reflected cloudy rainbows with her movements. Whatever mystical material it was composed of was also utilized in the creation of the long dress she wore, which dragged along behind her but failed to leave a trail in the sand. We were close, barely two feet apart, when she began to speak.

"You are Victoria Lindy Dinham."

It was not spoken as a question, but silence began unfurling between us, so I responded with an affirmative and she nodded pleasantly.

"Your brother wants me to thank you. This is from him." Her voice reminded me of the calm after a thunderstorm. She reached into her cloak and fiddled around as if trying to find something, then removed a single white carnation and held it out.

"My brother?" I asked incredulously, too taken aback to reach for the flower.

She looked a bit unsure with her arm still outstretched.

"Yes. He wanted to thank you for the stories and inform you that he's found a new kingdom."

Sleepless, nightmare-ridden nights that sent our prepubescent selves running to my closet, nicknamed The Kingdom, to read stories lurched into my memory. Those days were as dead as my father and reliving them didn't make things any easier.

Her patience seemed to be wearing thin. Either that or her arm was growing tired, so she took the flower and tucked it behind my ear.

"The stories," I began, ready to cross-examine some answers out of whoever this was, "How do you know about The Kingdom? Who are you?"

"Oh, I'm just a friend. A friend of your brother's, that is, although I have met you before. Admittedly, not as often as I'd like, but that's how it goes."

Was she kidding me? I finally get a dream with neither car accidents nor hospitals, and the star of it is a delusional stalker. Figures.

"I'm not taking that as an answer. Seriously, who are you?" I looked around at the unreal situation. Even asleep I knew there was no way to communicate with Reeves and decided just to cut to the chase.

Remembering something I had read once, I said, "This is a dream, correct? It's impossible to dream of someone you've never seen, and I know for a fact I've never met you before."

Endearing giggles slipped past her closed lips. "You're clever. I like you. How do you know you've never seen me before? Dreams are filled with random passersby you hardly even noticed on the street. You have a lifetime of unnoticed faces to work with."

"No, I'd remember you. I've never seen someone so perfect in all my life."

That wasn't a compliment; it was a fact. The girl looked like she could've walked off a cover for some sort of intergalactic edition of *Cosmopolitan* magazine. Her face lit up like a fireworks display.

"I'll take your word for it. If you must know, my name is Ashlinn and I create dreams. Your brother is happy and did, in fact, send me. That's all I'll disclose for now."

I nodded as if this was a perfectly normal thing to hear in everyday conversation, but my confusion was Titan-like in its enormity. She spoke of my brother as if he weren't comatose, but out there interacting. Living. Now, I may not have seen the car accident firsthand, but I knew the damage it had done wasn't easily reversible.

"I want proof," I said, like the star of some B action movie.

She raised an eyebrow at me and swung a foot in front of her, creating crescent moons in the sand.

"Proof? If that flower isn't proof enough once you awaken, then how about this: I know more about The Kingdom than what his message gave me to work with. The sandman, huh?"

My eyes grew so wide I might as well have been an animated princess. Ashlinn saw I wasn't going to be able to form sentences any time soon and threw in another comment.

"I must say I am flattered, especially considering *you* are the one so interested."

The waves were starting to sound even farther away than they had before, and she looked up at me.

"You're going to wake up soon. It has been nice meeting you. An absolute pleasure, even."

She nodded and turned to start walking off again, much in the way she had come, but before the fog could envelop her I reached out, shouting, "Wait!"

With my hand around her wrist, which felt almost insubstantial in my grasp, she turned back to me and lifted a questioning eyebrow.

"Let me see you again. Please."

At the time there was no good reason to have said it; the whole thing was completely impulsive, but looking back I could at least pretend I stopped her because she was my only connection to Reeves. I wanted so badly to believe there was a way to communicate with him. My brother was gone forever in my eyes, and if the amount of machinery they had hooked him up to couldn't bring him back, I was doubtful anything could get through, yet she delivered words he might have once thought. Even the hope of such a miracle was better than nothing.

She started shaking her head "no," and I released her wrist dejectedly, but then she sighed in frustration and growled.

"Fine. I'll see you tomorrow night as long as you try to tell yourself what just happened was only a dream, and the next one will coincidentally feature the same girl."

Before I could nod, the sand rushed away toward the direction of the ocean like an hourglass tilted sideways.

As the alarm clock screeched on my bedside table, I remembered having dreamed but was too exhausted to try and recall it completely at the moment. Only two thoughts swirled through my head: there was a girl in a magic cloak I had to see again, and nothing was more important than actually managing to get to sleep that night.

As I tumbled out of bed to begin preparing for the day, something fell from my head to the floor in front of me. I reached down blindly to pick it up, then turned on the lights.

A white carnation. Creamy petals that dented with a touch and a stem that could be marred by fingernails. Real.

It made me seven minutes late running out the door in the direction of my high school because of how long I spent trying to ensure its existence.

And if the bloom just happened to find its way into my bag there was no need to mention such a thing.

TWO

NO LAST day of school had ever felt so unimportant. The classes all passed in a daze of teachers showing irrelevant movies as my fellow students ignored each other in favor of trying not to pass out from heat exhaustion. Apparently most towns have high schools with functioning air-conditioning units. Yeah, I have never lived in one of those towns. With little else to occupy my mind throughout the classes, snippets of the dream began returning to me. Sand and sound and Her.

Ashlinn, that was her name. And there was something about Reeves. I tried to sort through these wisps of information with my forehead pressed against a desk, and found myself reaching into my bag to fiddle with the carnation, which was faring quite well in such a noxious environment.

The Kingdom.

Her comments, the absolute proof, resonated through my memory. It was such a casual reference but no one other than Reeves could possibly know. Whenever he couldn't sleep, or we wanted to hide from everything, he'd drag me in there. That closet was a universe of its own. It was always difficult to shut the doors from the inside, but we'd manage, and with flashlights propped up or dangling from clothes hangers, I'd read. There was a book of fables illustrated by someone who might as well have never even seen a pen, let alone known how to use one, and on nights Reeves awoke from nightmares I'd read him….

Damn.

I'd read him the story of the sandman.

No one mentioned when I groaned against the desk. What the hell had become of my life? I must admit, if Ashlinn was the sandman she beat every expectation. Due to the unimaginative illustrations of whoever-the-heck, I had always pictured the dude to be short and bearded. Maybe a bit pudgy. Definitely creepy. I'd take this version any day.

Like the alarm clock that pulled me away from her, school bells rang, and I exited the rooms without even bidding farewell to the teachers. Only two semesters and forty minutes left of high school with two short breaks for summers, and then it would be (hopefully) off to Manhattan.

But before any of that, I'd have to be social for a period.

I walked into class, giving a silent farewell to the poster of a cat saying "*Accrochez-vous*," and sat next to Ellie, who greeted me by groaning, "It's so hot I could tongue-kiss an air-conditioning unit. Not that we ever have any air-conditioning that actually works."

Like a swooning maiden, she had an arm flung across her forehead beneath her platinum white hair, which stood up in sweaty spikes. Her fashion sense could best be described as Burlesque Greaser, a fact she was probably lamenting, considering how pleather was never famed for its cooling properties.

Madame Velsh put on the second half of some French cartoon called *Astérix*, which everyone in the class ignored as she stressed over entering all of our grades into the computer, a system the old woman never really understood. My friend shifted next to me, uncomfortable in the heat.

"I found a tattoo parlor. I'm gonna call them up the next time my parents are out and schedule the first appointment to make my design. Sure you don't wanna come?" Ellie spoke with her eyes closed, languidly stretched out beneath the desk, but there was no doubt the inquiry was for me, judging by how many times she had asked similar things in the past month alone.

"You don't need me there," I told her. "What design are you planning to get?"

"The Jersey Devil," she informed me with a smile in her voice.

Well, that was unexpected.

"Why?"

"He's gonna be my protector when I go off to college. When I was little, I thought he lived right outside my window, but I wasn't frightened. He watched out for me, scared away the real monsters. So maybe having him on my thigh forever will keep away more than some werewolves."

"I'm not sure if anything is gonna scare away drunken frat boys."

She snorted and went back to fake napping.

We didn't talk about college often. Generally schoolwork was an unsafe topic around Ellie, not because she hated it but because she was a genius. Her grades were so good she felt guilty for not having to try too hard. She had several reputations with varying cliques and clubs throughout the school, and the only friends who might have had any idea of her brilliance were those gained in AP government and chemistry. The rest of the school remained in blissful ignorance of the fact she was in those classes at all, and the only reason I was privy to this knowledge was because of how close we were. Well, used to be. Before the accident.

At the end of class, she leaned over my desk.

"Hey, it's the last day of school. Why don't you let me drive you home in The Hovercraft?"

Another fact about Ellie is that she lovingly referred to her old green Dodge as The Hovercraft. The car had been passed down through two older brothers and her father before them, and once when she was younger, one brother in particular said that by the time she got her license everyone else would be floating up to school in a hovercraft. She would still be stuck in their piece of crap car. She believed every word and was petrified of how much everyone would mock her for rolling around on wheels while they flew. When the last brother in the parade of those before her passed over the keys, she gave the car its current moniker in spite of his prediction, and it stuck. That was of her own doing, though.

I really didn't feel like walking. It was warmer than the heart of Saint Nick out there and driving cut transportation time. I could definitely do with the extra minutes to think about last night and the reason why there was a white flower wedged between the pages of my English notebook, so I accepted her offer. Ellie looked painfully surprised. We walked out of class together, and I almost forgot we barely spoke anymore, not since last year, and made a show of not having to stop at our lockers. In fact, she leaned against them as we walked, dragging her backpack along so everyone could hear the click of the zipper against each lock.

The atmosphere was absolutely buoyant and the seniors might have just floated away if they got any giddier. That would be us in a year's time.

Ellie cheerily waved to a good chunk of the school's population, and you could see the different nuances in each greeting depending on the image she maintained with that group of people. It was an impressive, if subtle, feat. By the time we reached her car, she had shouted to so many students to have a "fantastic fucking summer" that it was shocking she hadn't gone hoarse.

I slouched into the passenger's seat as she took the driver's position, grinning.

"Let's go get ice cream or something. It's our last day in that hellhole for two months, and we gotta celebrate."

"I haven't got any money." The truth. "And I'm not too keen on ice cream anymore." A lie.

She reached over me to grab sunglasses out of the glove compartment.

"No worries, I'll cover you. I'm not sure what ice cream ever did to you, but we can get fries instead. Let's go."

Ellie donned the glasses with a grin that showed she definitely realized how cool she looked before rocketing out of the parking lot as fast as one could go without drawing the attention of any security guards.

We both stared out the front windshield, and before the silence could become oppressive she started playing a CD. She sang along loudly with some song from the sixties called "Green Tambourine." Her words were definitely incorrect. When it finally ended, the song began again without giving me any break.

"Are there any other songs on this disc?" I asked, confused.

"Nah. It's not even mine, really. It was Kevin's, that guy I dated back in October so I could buy those cute Halloween costumes. The sort for couples. He was obsessed with this song and made a CD of nothing but the damn thing on repeat. Been too lazy to take it out, so now I'm an expert on the intricacies of a song, which honestly sounds like the result of an acid trip. My every dream come true."

It was like a pro wrestling match. In one corner: awkward silence and small talk with someone who used to know every detail of your life. In the other: a god-awful song that generates headaches like it was being paid to. Which one was more painful? I opted to stick with the headaches, so it played on as an old road carried us in the opposite direction of my house and toward McDonald's.

"I'm gonna try and bring us through the drive-thru. Let's see how badly I fuck it up."

She swung the wheel around dramatically and ended up a bit too far from where we ordered, but that could be dealt with by shouting loudly into the voice box. When she pulled around again we ended up even farther away from the building than before. The zombie-like employee seemed almost on the verge of being amused when Ellie was forced to climb out of the car and walk up to the window to take the food. She hopped back in after giving a wave to those in line behind us, carrying bags that bulged with greasy fries.

"This is why we should all be like you and avoid driving. I don't know what I did to pass my test, but someone out there is regretting it now." She was smiling, but that began to melt away when she glanced at me.

My mind had jumped back to Reeves and Dad.

Shards of metal and rivers of gas. Hospital beds and freshly dug graves.

Why the hell was I in a car if that's what killed my family? The air in them always seemed several sizes too small for my lungs.

Ellie looked at me, panicked. She didn't seem as oxygen deprived as it felt in this damn car.

"Shit, I'm sorry. That was a really insensitive thing to say. Shouldn't have brought that up, the whole driving thing. You okay?"

I just nodded and faked a smile as she handed over the food and began driving away. I rolled down the window halfway and rested my head against it.

"Yeah I'm fine."

That response was delayed, and I don't think she bought it. The somewhat jovial mood was gone. She acted just as upbeat as before, though, and soon said, "Fry me," opening her mouth and leaning toward me with eyes still on the road. Getting the message, I pried my hands off her car door and shoved four fries between her teeth. I ate mine quietly beside her, and we listened to "Green Tambourine" yet again and after this time, simultaneously the fourth hearing of it that day and in my whole life, she clicked it off.

"Okay, I dished out one of my infamous idiotic ex stories about the CD. Please tell me you've managed to get a few for yourself recently. Any chance you've found a girlfriend and have just been really good at hiding it from me?" Her tone was eager, if not a bit exasperated.

Having her knowledgeable of my sexuality should have been a blessing, but I almost wished she was as clueless as the rest of the school. I never even came out of the closet. She more or less dragged me and had refused to keep quiet about it since. The thought of being in a relationship wasn't distasteful; I just didn't feel ready. My excuse was always that I was waiting until after high school, but she didn't buy that and was constantly trying to push me into the arms of lesbians or even men that, in her words, were "feminine enough that I shouldn't mind too much." Instead of going off on her for pressuring me or breaking the news that I wasn't even sure of my sexuality, I told a variation of the truth.

"Sorry to disappoint. If I had a girlfriend, you'd be the first to know."

She turned to glare at me over the top of her sunglasses.

"You're going to be the only person in college who has no idea how to make out with someone."

How does one go about telling her friend that she didn't seem to have grown out of the kissing-is-icky phase we spent our whole youth in? People really enjoyed kissing—that was one fact of life—so obviously I believed I would enjoy it too one day, but I wasn't in the mood to hurry it along. If movies had taught me one thing, it was that this could wait for college. I just shrugged at her statement and stared out the window, my thoughts scattering like dandelion fuzz but now rooted in Ashlinn. Remembering the accident reminded me of Reeves. That girl knew about the stories I had once told my brother. How was that possible?

We were nearing my house. Thank God. Ellie was wonderful, but people change. I had witnessed this firsthand with her, but that fact was starting to become even more applicable to me. The Hovercraft pulled to the curb, and I said a quick good-bye before jumping out. As I walked away, she rolled down the window and shouted, "Hey, are you doing anything tonight? I'm having a bonfire with some friends later."

"Which ones, the honors society members or the stoners?"

Her brilliant smile faltered but only for a blip in time. "Oh, none of them. Just some guys from my study hall."

The last time I had willingly spent free time with someone my age had happened over a year ago. All the excuses that sprang to the forefront of my mind were weak, so I just threw one that had worked in the past, well aware that she probably wouldn't buy it.

"Sorry, but I have to practice my dance."

At that her already weak smile turned sad. "Yeah, don't you always? Catch you around, Victoria." She pushed the sunglasses farther up on her nose, and I heard the beginnings of "Green Tambourine" through the window as she pulled away.

The second I got in the house, I took the carnation from my bag and tucked it back behind my ear, then tossed the bag in the coat closet. That wouldn't be needed for a whole season.

Walking into the living room revealed Mother passed out asleep on the couch with her shoes (and the TV) still on. I tapped her on the shoulder, and she shuddered awake with panic seizing her body ┕   hen she settled drowsily after a second.

"   I didn't mean to fall asleep. What time is it?" she

             hands over her face and sitting up straighter on

             ice flower," she added, squinting at my head,

             rter to three." I pointed at the clock on the
             off the couch.

             the hospital before you came home!
             er soon." She ran to her purse and

rummaged around for the keys, then turned to me like a whirlwind and asked doubtfully, "Wanna come?"

Instead of responding with the impulsive Absolutely Not and giving the same excuse I had just told Ellie, I stopped myself. It was impossible to think of Reeves passively. When he came to mind, there was no option but to devote all my energy to drowning in regret, so my fallback was to just ignore the whole thing, as awful as that sounds. After last night's dream, though, it felt wrong. Even if he hadn't sent me a message, my mind had decided that his existence needed to be addressed. Maybe seeing him was what I needed.

Steeling myself, I told my mother I would join her, and her eyes widened, looking just as surprised as I felt.

We drove in a familiar silence. I hadn't visited Reeves since it became clear he wouldn't be getting any better, and I remembered why as we pulled up outside the hospital. At the graveyard there was no hope, so there was nothing to lose and no chance for disappointment. Optimists could only be let down.

Driving twice in a day was a bit extreme for me, so I just closed my eyes and mapped out dance moves, chewing my cheek the whole ride there.

The gates and flowers outside seemed infinitely more foreboding than the ones I was used to seeing, but Mother was immune to them. She walked the sterile halls with intent, and it was obvious she knew her way through the twisting corridors just as well as I could navigate the churchyard. Where this was a walk she took often, I was not accustomed to the place. Beeping monitors and rolling carts were the only sounds of life.

The walls were so white they were practically reflective, and as we neared the long-term-care unit I could feel my breathing pick up speed with every step. It was starting to seem ridiculous that a dream made me feel so compelled to look at my brother.

As we neared the door to his room, I tried not to allow my steps to falter. Stoicism prevailed, and I walked on as if my brain was screaming at me to run in the other direction. We finally and saw him lying there. He looked different than I which shouldn't have been so shocking consider him in pictures for the past twelve months, but the thought was still a heartbreaking one. On those rare occasions I reflected on the past, I had always assumed his face was correct in my memory. If I couldn't even get that right, who knows what I had butchered about his personality.

Perhaps it was because of his calm visage. In every image I had of him, he was in action and smiling. Now he was emotionless with unwavering lips. He was nestled between white sheets on top of a white pillow, and they seemed to drain him of color he lacked to begin with. The hospital made it look like we were lost in a whiteout snowstorm, which was actually a pretty accurate description of how I felt. Everything was devoid of color from the walls to the nurses, and if he was ever to miraculously awaken, I feared he would think himself among the colorless clouds of heaven.

Mother walked up to him as I remained motionless in the doorway. So much for stoicism. She put her thumb on his chin, then straightened the already pristine sheets, which had probably not been altered much since her last visit. There was a chair next to the bed (not white, I noted gratefully) and she dropped herself into it so violently it almost seemed like she was pushed. Her hand reached out and just lay on the bed as I took a tentative step toward Reeves.

My shoes were thunderous against the floor, so I quickened my pace and closed the distance. I stood by his feet and felt the need to make certain there was heat coming off his skin and that he wasn't just frozen in time. Not wanting to move Mother's hand, I skittered around to the opposite side of the bed and gently took his pulse with two fingers to the neck, hoping it appeared to just be an affectionate touch. Satisfied with the feel of his heartbeat's echo, I placed my hand on his forehead, then brought it around to his cheek. All evidence was pointing in the direction of him being the same as before. He'd have been so excited today, it being the last day of school and all, and he couldn't even quirk a smile.

Glancing over at Mother made it obvious she had gotten lost in her head; she was gazing up at the ceiling as if it held the answers to everything. While she stared at the tiles, I bent over and whispered in his ear, offering a thank-you for the carnation.

We had been there only ten minutes when a sickeningly kind nurse came and told us visiting hours were over. Her smile was full of straight white teeth and pity I hadn't earned. She flashed us those teeth while shooing us out of the room, taking my mother's place at Reeves's side.

The ride home was as silent as the one there had been, but this time there was an air of unpleasantness. Mother was emotionally drained, and I felt just as haggard. When I stepped inside the house, the carnation fell from behind my ear to the floor and lost two petals. Leaving them on the floor, I picked it up and went upstairs, where I placed it on my bedside table permanently.

The whole ordeal at the hospital probably had given me dark circles under my eyes. I never danced that night, making what I had told Ellie a lie, and I imagined what she'd be doing at the bonfire as I stared at my ceiling and willed sleep to come.

THREE

WHEN I entered the dream, every memory of Ashlinn and our short meeting returned, but the clarity of those thoughts clashed with the haziness of the abstract world around me. It looked oddly familiar, but there seemed to be a block in my head preventing the memories from clicking into place. I was in a decrepit old theater with red velvet seats and gold filigree. The seats, upon closer inspection, were matted and full of small tears and God knew what else. Any paint was now chipped off the walls and reincarnated as a thick layer of dust on the floor. The stage was a void, just a pitch-black rectangle every aisle led to, and looking up revealed a lack of the usual necessary lighting equipment.

Perched on one of the seats was a glimmering shadow and I recognized the cloak immediately. She didn't even twitch when I ran right in front of her, much more quickly than I would have in reality—it was more like I wanted to be by her and then simply was—and asked sharply, "How the hell did you know those things about Reeves? He's unconscious. I should know; I saw him today."

Up until this point she had been staring straight ahead, but now she glanced up and her eyes met mine. There was so much life in them. Too much.

"He'll be glad you visited. I'll be sure to tell him. Right now I want to talk about you, though. It's not every day I pay someone a repeat visit, lucky girl. Come along."

That was one way to talk around a question.

She stood up, the seat folding back in on itself slowly, and then she squeezed past me where I stood half in the aisle, half in the row, and headed toward the stage. I followed unquestioningly, almost with a will that wasn't my own. With a hop that wouldn't have been feasible in the waking world, she was able to seat herself on the edge of the stage with legs dangling, and I followed suit because it felt like the proper, if not only, thing to do.

This new perspective revealed how expansive the theater was, with a balcony and everything. I was surveying the room and absorbing the setting, trying desperately to remember how I knew of it. There were echoes of laughter when Ashlinn's voice broke through my confused reverie.

"You are not frightened."

She was correct. There was a dark emptiness behind us and the whole building was dipped in a surreal sort of creepiness. Now that I knew terror should be present, I expected it to begin encroaching any second, to float in among the giggles as it should, yet the placid serenity remained.

"Why?" I asked with genuine curiosity.

"I composed this for you out of a happy memory. You were not scared when you visited this place the first time, so there's no reason for you to be frightened now. Do you know where you are?"

"Yes. Well, no. It's really irritating. I know I should remember, but it's just not coming."

"In dreams one has selective memories of life outside of them, same as how in reality you rarely recall dreams. Recent events, such as your visit with Reeves today, should still be lurking about, but oftentimes it's harder to bring back the past. The last time you were here was before Reeves became a permanent resident in my realm. It might do you well to go back someday."

"If you've really been talking to Reeves, you should know what I've been dealing with. I'm not sure if visiting this place is really a priority."

Ashlinn's demeanor switched in a flash to a charmingly embarrassed one. She spoke slowly.

"Actually, I don't know what happened to Reeves. I do two things. One is that I catch people who dream they are falling. If you get that tipsy feeling when you turn over in bed, I'm the one stopping it. My second ability is that I can sort through someone's happy memories and hopes, then spin those into a dream. I doubt it's a very happy memory, so I've never been able to see it in you, and he doesn't know. Only Semira knows, and she refuses to spill the beans."

"Semira?"

"Makes the nightmares, kind of like the antiversion of me, but she isn't a bad woman. We're getting off topic, though," she continued in a tone of false reluctance. "Care to tell me what happened to Reeves? He's pretty curious himself."

She had said earlier that old memories remained dormant in dreams, yet that one burned brightly at the forefront of my mind.

"I thought this was supposed to be a good dream," I mumbled, trying to delay.

"I just make the cheerful settings and inhabit them. The decisions are up to you, dearie."

I wasn't sure if I wanted the decisions. She was swinging her legs against the stage in large circles and occasionally brushing against mine, so I began mimicking her and our feet were like two cogs, spinning onward for eternity.

"This seems like something I should be discussing with a therapist, and God knows that hasn't worked out. Honestly, this is one of the freakiest things to have happened to me in a while. I don't even know who you are or if I believe what you said about Reeves. I'm not about to bare my soul to you."

Even as I said this, a small part of me was contradictory and desired to tell her everything. Maybe it was the ease of not being in reality, where the world was nothing but attacks and harsh edges. All friends acted like therapists. I didn't get that vibe from Ashlinn, though, and it was tempting to finally free myself and speak not just about losing my father and brother, but about how terrified I was of not getting into dance school and that tingle of anxiety every time I rode in a car, and ask her about her fears as well. If she had any, that is.

Out of the corner of my eye, I could see she was nodding at my statement, unoffended, and I decided it was time for me to find out a bit about her. I hopped off the stage and stood in front of her, gazing up as she tilted her head downward.

Ashlinn was clinging to every word. "When she is home, she's empty, dwelling on the day it all happened, sorta like what I do. Hopefully I don't seem as miserable as her on the outside. But we're hanging in there. Honestly, we don't talk much anymore."

Ashlinn looked stricken. "I think I'll just tell him the first bit, about her being great."

I nodded in accordance. That was probably for the best.

That devastated look would not leave her face. It was obvious she was fond of me for some unknown reason, but this sadness seemed oddly intense considering she felt like a stranger.

"Victoria, I...," she said, reaching out to me, but I turned my face from her with an upraised hand.

"Don't."

She nodded and gently asked, "And what of your father?"

Don't make me say it.

"Dead," I croaked out toward the floor. She gasped.

"I visit his grave every week. Reeves wasn't the only one we lost that day." I turned my head up toward her.

"I am so sorry—"

"I don't want to talk about it please. And—" I stopped, ashamed of what I wanted to ask her to do for me. It would have been nice to demand she not tell Reeves, so he could remain in blissful ignorance, but that just wouldn't be fair. If he were out there somewhere, he deserved to know the truth. Actually, so did I.

"You know what? Never mind. But now that I've answered your question," I continued, with some deserved ire, "will you please tell me how the hell you're talking to my brother?"

She was obviously still upset from hearing about my father's mortality. That got to us all. It made me wonder what she had heard of him from Reeves. I wished I hadn't stopped her from reaching out to me. It was just her pitying words I had been attempting to cut off.

Ashlinn was obviously reluctant to answer my question but seemed to feel a bit guilty.

"Okay, your brother has been in a coma for a little over a year, asleep. I'm not sure if you've figured out what I do yet, but you must have deduced that I can wander through dreams. To be more precise, I create the dreams." She took a break and I nodded for her to continue.

"When I look at the sleeping mind of a human being, their happy memories, aspirations, and wishes float to the top, and I make situations out of them. Settings in which their minds can work out whatever the day threw at them. Now that you know what I do, it can't be too difficult a leap to figure out how I have been communicating with your brother. He has little else to do but live in the worlds I create for him. We're actually quite close, and he has said marvelous things about you. Definitely meeting expectations up to this point, dearie. There are blank spots in his memory, but you're in many of the snatches of his past I've had the privilege to work with."

I didn't even want to start thinking about what memories she had seen, but apparently they had to have been nice ones. If her words hadn't been so shocking, maybe I would have been able to appreciate how low her voice was. Those were the most words I'd heard her speak thus far. Ashlinn was her voice: sedate and calm, an oasis from our explosive world with its sobs and clattering metals.

"So you make the good dreams?"

"Not exactly. I just knit together the nice backgrounds and fill them with people. You guys dictate the rest of it."

I remembered what she had said last night about The Kingdom. "Are you really the sandman? That was one of the stories I used to tell Reeves when he was younger. He adored it. The man who gave children beautiful dreams with a rainbow umbrella."

I looked accusingly into the seat next to me at the parasol she still had on her arm, now propped up on the armrest of another chair.

"I'm not a man, and I have yet to get involved with any sand. Well, apart from the beaches I bring people to, as you should recall. Reeves asked me a similar question. Whoever wrote that tale probably based it on me." She sounded charmed, verging on smug.

"That story has got to be centuries old. Aren't you a teenager?"

She looked like a sixteen-year-old, with flawless dark skin and no sign of any wrinkles. Again I lamented the hood as I couldn't see the color of her hair but had every confidence in it not being gray.

"I have no idea. Time passes differently in dreams. How else would you be able to fit so much in one night? It's been a while since I've looked in a mirror, but not much has been changing for as long as I can remember."

There was so much to ask her. The more questions she answered the more they inspired. Queries were popping up like daffodils in my mind, but before I could ask another she clapped her hands as if to signal a subject change.

"So," she exclaimed loudly, interrupting any words I was about to speak, "we are in a theater with a wonderful stage, and I have been reliably informed that you are a ballerina. Now, I have a certain affinity for watching ballet. Dance a little something for me. We should have time." Her demeanor shifted, and excitement brimmed in her voice and gestures.

Someone was definitely looking for a diversion. Too bad she also seemed extremely genuine.

"I don't have my outfit or my music, and that stage is pitch black."

She almost seemed disappointed in my excuses, like she expected me to do better. With a snap of those elegant fingers, every qualm I had voiced was attended to, and I looked down to see skin-tone pointe shoes, much nicer than my actual pair, already tied on with ribbons crisscrossing over nylon-sheathed legs. There was a leotard composed of the same fabric as her dress, and likewise it couldn't decide on a color. Looking up revealed the stage to be brightly lit, although the source of such light was a mystery, and it was pristine. Far too new in comparison to the rest of the building.

"What about the music?" I asked in a last-ditch effort to avoid performing for an audience of one extremely distracting individual.

"You don't need it."

She pushed me out of the chair and toward the stage while extending her own legs out to recline.

The shoes were so comfortable it was actually alarming. The pain that came with pointe was worrisome but grounding, and I had the veins to prove it. Now I could hardly even tell there was anything on my feet.

At first I inched toward the stage, feeling exposed in my outfit, even though I often donned less in front of much larger crowds. Determined not to make a fool of myself, my steps became more sure as I trod up the three stairs to the stage. Ashlinn gave me an encouraging thumbs-up from where she sat.

God, I was about to perform for the freaking sandman.

Who was probably magical.

And may or may not have a crush on me.

It really shouldn't have been too much of a surprise that I began making excuses for what she was about to witness, even though my dancing was the one thing I felt confident about.

"I only have about twenty seconds choreographed, and it's gonna look really stupid without the music. I'm working on it now for my conservatory auditions, which aren't for another two weeks, so I have reason enough to not be done."

I was babbling, but the words wouldn't cease. My voice might not even have been reaching her side of the theater. Thankfully, she interrupted me.

"I'm sure it's fantastic, and if it isn't, rest assured that I've seen worse. Just dance before the morning interrupts this lovely date."

Date?

I closed my eyes, pretending I was preparing to dance, but honestly my brain just needed to recuperate from her last statement. Every thought was ringing with the word *date* on repeat, and I could only hope that my nervousness over that single syllable wasn't overly apparent. I took a deep breath and began.

With fluid motions my legs carried me over the stage, and silence permeated the air save for my footfalls.

Am I ready to date? What if she expects me to kiss her?

My eyes met the ceiling and the walls, but I never dared to look down to the seats below.

Do I even really know her? She seems to know me.

With liquid arms I went up into my first arabesque, and then they became rigid with downturned elbows as my leg lifted up behind me.

She isn't even real.

Balance. I already felt idiotic without the music guiding every step, and my movements seemed increasingly inelastic without the external notes to focus on.

The dance continued, and I transitioned into a chassé. My mind kept wandering to who was watching me, and I was struck once again with the realization that she had called this a date, something I had never experienced before and obviously did not know how to handle. Like a self-fulfilling prophecy, my feet faltered and I fell to the black floor.

The stage was even beneath my hands, unnaturally so. There were no ridges or bumps, and it was impossible to differentiate the planks of wood. The paint was perfectly intact with no sign of any chipping, which just didn't seem right. Kneeling on the stage, I lifted my palms expecting them to be inlaid with grit, but they were perfectly clean. This whole scenario was horrifying, something that could send anyone sane into a fit of wheezing, but before any such hysterics could begin, I found myself prostrated before a shadow.

My gaze crept up from the floor and toward Ashlinn, who was reaching out for me. The golden light around her was so bright it masked her face and every expression on it, leaving her disappointment to the imagination.

When did she get on stage?

I moved to start standing on my own when she lunged forward and grabbed both of my hands, hauling me up. We tottered backward but managed to remain upright.

"Sorry," I murmured, staring at where she held my limp hands.

"What for?" she asked, as if it weren't obvious.

"I mean, I messed up."

"Messed up?" she said with impressively feigned confusion. "Why, I thought it was all part of the performance. A signal for me to cut in."

With that, she repositioned my hands onto her waist while hers found its way to my shoulder. Before I even knew what was happening she began dragging me around like a whirlwind, and I finally understood what Dorothy made all the fuss about at the start of *The Wizard of Oz*. I half expected to see a woman on a bike fly by. My confused feet followed along. If they hadn't, I surely would have been dragged. She was moving backward in circles, leading me over every inch of the stage.

And I was laughing. Giddy bursts of giggles that made my ribs ache from the inside, but there was no stopping this girl.

"What kind of dancing is this?" I managed to get out between silent snorts.

She hummed, looking down at our feet as if trying to figure it out herself. "I'd say it's a mix between square and tango. Let's fix that."

She released one of my hands, spinning me out dizzily as a human yo-yo.

"How do you feel about swing?" she asked, pulling me back in and reclaiming both my hands, except this time my back was to her front.

"Ambiguous, I guess."

"Let's make you love it, then. Time to Charleston." She lightly tapped the back of my right foot with her own and, getting the message, I kicked up my own leg as hers followed, although not nearly as high. Remembering the old Hollywood musicals I had once been enamored with, I stepped back with my left foot and, thankfully, didn't land on her toes. We were moving as one, arms working like the wheels of a train. It had been so long since I'd danced anything other than the precise moves of ballet, where perfection was the sole endgame. That was necessary, like the blood flowing from my heart to my head, but this was more. This was fun.

Ashlinn's voice came from behind me, bringing on the realization that this was the first time I had danced with a partner in God knows how long, and she wasn't even out of breath. Well, neither was I.

"I'd throw you between my legs like the professionals, but I think this dress would get in the way, so we'll just have to make do with this."

Without further ado, she stopped her kicking and grabbed my waist, and before any protestations could be made, I was being hurled into the air. As I floated out of her arms, practically parallel to the ceiling, the dream unfurled around me. Consciousness began to sap away the hazy quality and drag me into drab reality, but I could swear there was applause, and maybe even a whispered thank-you.

Oh, Ashlinn, you're so welcome.

FOUR

SUNLIGHT HIT my eyelids, and I blinked my eyes open blearily. The only thoughts rolling around in my skull had to do with the old theater in town where I had my dance recitals until it was closed for good and abandoned. Ellie and I sneaked in there once a few years later, one summer morning before our teenage years had taught us fear.

Groaning angrily, I rolled over so my back was toward the window. A dream. I definitely had a dream. I closed my eyes yet again, not expecting to get any more sleep, but after a few seconds, they shot open as I began recalling what had happened just before waking.

Ashlinn. I remembered her and how she grinned like the Cheshire cat. We had a date. Holy shit. I went on a date in a dream with a mildly mythical figure who couldn't possibly exist. And we were swing dancing. I silently applauded my imagination for its overactivity last night.

It was the first day of summer, and I had nothing going on. There was a desire to not move out of bed all day, which was starting to seem more likely as I heard Mother walking around downstairs. The floors and walls did little to block the noises in the house, instead just adding to them with their own creaks and groans, and I could hear her high-heeled shoes click on the kitchen's tile floors. Not wishing to make small talk, I decided to stay in bed until the garage door opened and closed, signaling her exit. As I lay there listening to her rustling, I did my best to recall the dream. Images like puzzle pieces scrambled themselves in my memory.

A collage of dancing and gold filigree and laying my hands on her waist. We had spoken of Reeves. I almost began to accept that I'd finally gone round the bend and this was my mind's way of pretending my brother wasn't as much of a goner as my father. My ex-therapist had said we all deal with grief in different ways. Maybe mine was manifesting itself as a fantasy world in my head. One where coma patients could send messages through flirty dream makers.

This was turning into a bit of a crisis.

Eventually the garage door opened, and I heard the faint sound of a car engine as my mother pulled out of the driveway and onto the main street. I threw my comforter off and slumped out of the plush haven, not even bothering to make the bed afterward.

A carnation was drying on my bedside table.

The first order of business would be to don my bathrobe and go to the kitchen where I would sit around for a ridiculous amount of time drinking tea, and after that luxury was complete, I intended to think about the day and what it would hold for me. I went about my missions.

The tea was strong, and I added too much sugar to counteract that, yet drank the whole pot while staring into our small rectangle of a backyard. It hadn't rained in days, and the flowers were wilting.

Without even bothering to put on shoes, I abandoned the tea and stepped out onto the lawn to start watering the plants in my pajamas and bathrobe, grateful that there was a marginally tall fence surrounding the property. The roots greedily accepted what dripped and sputtered out of our hose, and I doused them accordingly, maybe even too much. This time of the year was always nice; all of the flowers were already in the earth and the only thing left was to provide them with sustenance. The small patch of carnations caught my eye, and as I focused on a white one, my mind began wandering back to Ashlinn.

She seemed like such an affectionate person. Couldn't we just stick to that? Going further was something I'd managed to put off for all of high school, and I wasn't too keen to break that record yet. She seemed to be offering me her adoration, but what she'd want in return was troubling. This wasn't something that happened to people like me; it's something that happened in movies.

I had had the same thoughts over a year ago when the police officer showed up at the door, but this situation was much more amenable.

That day passed in the way so many had before it, except there was no schoolwork taking up the first six hours of my consciousness. I practiced my dance for ages and, when not doing that, pretended I knew how to cook. In the afternoon I began preparing my portfolio for the audition, filling a manila folder with my alarmingly white résumé and ten-dollar headshot.

After Mother returned home and made dinner, we watched TV until I made my exit for the night. She made no comment about how she didn't have to force me into bed for once in her life. I went willingly, with the foolish hope that Ashlinn would return to sate my curiosity, and my hopes were somewhat achieved.

When the dream began, it seemed as if I was already in the middle of a conversation. Blue light and glass surrounded me, but there was little time to notice this. Ashlinn was walking, and I was right alongside her.

"So you were talking about auditions. Where are you trying to go to college?"

She spoke as if we had been discussing the matter for hours beforehand. I stared at her, elusive and ethereal, as my feet carried me along. I wished to link my arm through hers. Contact was definitely a craving, but what else? I tried to imagine going further, doing the things that Ellie often spoke of, but felt nothing. There wasn't revulsion, but a distinct disinterest. After a few seconds, I realized she had asked a question and I tried to get back on track.

"I have an audition with the Manhattan Dance Conservatory in something like ten days. Mother's gonna drive me up to the city. If I don't get in, I'm screwed."

"Can't you go to a different college? You must have a fallback. Who plans only one audition?"

This was the same question my guidance counselor had asked me. Figuring my lack of desire to do anything to further myself recently wouldn't go over well as an excuse, I dragged out the same thing I told school personnel.

"It's the only decent one I'd be able to afford. There's good financial aid, and it's close enough to home that Mother won't be completely abandoned. If I don't get in, there's always community college, which isn't too bad. I mean, lots of people from school go, and they won't be turning me down for my crappy SATs, but they don't offer degrees in the arts. I'm not good at much else apart from dancing, so I don't know what I'll do if this doesn't work out."

"If the ballet I saw is anything to go by, I think you have more than a fair chance."

We were walking closer now, with arms brushing occasionally, and I finally began to observe the room around us. There were great glass windows stretching up into infinity and behind them, a rainbow. Coral spread out across the floor like a turgid garden, and fish darted about among them, painting the water with their streaked scales.

"An aquarium?" I asked, forgetting the fears of the previous moment.

She hummed in acquiescence.

"It's hard not to like an ocean you can walk through without drowning."

A dolphin was beginning to career its way through the water, and I ran up to the glass.

"It's so peaceful. Do you think they're happy?"

Her voice came from behind me. "They aren't real."

"Spoilsport. Even if they aren't real you still are." I turned back to her and leaned against the tank.

"I am not imaginary, but I could be lying in saying that. It might just be your brain making up these words and me along with them."

My head was shaking before she had even finished her sentence.

"We already covered the fact that I'm not good for much apart from dancing. I'm not creative or smart, and I definitely couldn't have thought up someone like you. Besides, you let me have the flower. I think you want me to believe."

"While I can't disagree with that, I can say that you are wrong about your intelligence. Dancing is very creative and few people would be smart enough to figure out that this is all real. You, my dear, simply can't be restricted by letters on a report card."

Is it possible to blush in a dream? I hope not because I would have been the winner of a Hellboy look-alike contest. No one had ever said anything like that to me before. In school negative remarks were as common as my poor grades, and even at home my parents had always been harsh about schoolwork. Now my mother was harsh about nothing because she wasn't enthusiastic about anything either. The strange thing was, I wasn't sure if I wanted to get used to Ashlinn's kindness. Being pleasantly surprised nightly wasn't a bad thing.

Once again I turned away from Ashlinn so she wouldn't see how much her kind words had affected me, but she seemed to sense something was amiss. I was in the middle of a staring contest with a deflated puffer fish when her apparitional fingers grabbed my shoulder.

"What's wrong?"

How could I tell her that something was changing? She held the key to those dusty cabinets of my mind, and doors were flinging open left and right. I didn't feel obliged to mince words or talk around everything anymore. Maybe it was her and the dream state compelling me to be more open. Maybe I had finally found someone I trusted enough to be open with, even so early in our relationship.

"Nothing. I just really like you is all, and I don't see how that could ever work out."

I could practically feel her unasked questions and decided to save her the pain.

"Obviously you know I'm a lesbian," I began, not meeting her eyes. "You are in my head after all, and that fact hasn't been particularly kind to me."

She was staring at me.

"Actually I didn't know you were a lesbian."

Shit. I stuttered through excuses.

"Oh God, I shouldn't have told you that. Please don't leave forever. I know it's only the third time we've seen each other and I should be a bit more freaked out with you being in my head and all, but it's less lonely with you up there." It was like the constricting car ride with Ellie all over again.

She cut me off with a placating gesture.

"I'm not leaving forever. You know I can only see happy memories. Those are what good dreams are composed of. Obviously you aren't exactly proud of your sexuality because that doesn't make the cut of pleasant things in your mind. What happened to you?"

I still feared scaring her away but remembered the way she had been flirting with me if that's what it really was. We were past the point of no return already, so I might as well keep going.

"Whenever I imagined my future, growing up and getting married, for some reason I always pictured a woman. It was just how my mind worked. It was always a wife. I tried to look at guys and will them to be hot, but it didn't happen, not that it really happened much with girls either. I mean, I can tell when someone is attractive and I appreciate it, but I've yet to grasp the whole sexiness thing, but that's whatever. So once I told Ellie about the whole wife thing, 'cause that's what you do, isn't it? Talk through your sexuality crises with friends? I only got about a sentence in when she just said 'That means you're a lesbian,' and I went along with it. I mean, she's right, isn't she?"

I looked up imploringly at Ashlinn. Her hand, which had been resting on my shoulder, fell away. I felt the shame begin creeping up in earnest, but my soul was saved when her fingers returned and laced in mine. My eyebrows were raised and my mouth was wide open, but she just nodded with an understanding expression.

"You know your sexuality isn't set in stone. There are more things than just gay or straight. It might be time you start exploring those."

"Wish you coulda told her that."

"Maybe I will one day. Now I'm not so sure how I feel about this friend who forces lesbianism upon people. She always seemed cool to me. I'm disappointed."

The thought of her meeting Ellie didn't have a place in my mind. They were as different as two people could be. Ashlinn was ice where Ellie was fire. They were lace panties to boxer shorts, Easter to Halloween.

"I promise she's not all that bad. She thrives on social justice and defending minorities and all that. We were actually best friends for, well, ever. At each other's houses every weekend growing up. We only stopped being so damn close a year ago."

"Sounds to me like you've been pushing people away."

"Well I'm not pushing you away."

As I said those words, I realized how true they were. Ashlinn was the first person I had made an effort with in ages, and it took me that long to even notice. I wanted to talk to her; she was an explosion in a silent film, subdued yet powerful. Realizing my words, I began talking again.

"And she was always a bit too intense for me anyway. We stopped fitting together so well once we made it to high school. Losing Dad and Reeves was just the clincher."

"Intense?" Ashlinn asked, although I'm not sure if she was really as intrigued in the subject manner as she was pretending to be.

"Yeah. I mean, one time last year, she went missing. Her parents got the police involved and everything. They hunted for an entire day. Turns out she had seen this rally for vegetarianism or something online and decided to drive to Texas and help them. She did this in the middle of the night without telling anyone. They found her asleep in her car in a Walmart parking lot the next day. She had gotten all the way to western Pennsylvania."

"And she's still free to do things?"

"Her parents could care less as long as her grades stay so fantastic."

I tried to school the jealousy out of my tone. Not only did Ellie have parents plural, but Yale-worthy test scores.

"They're probably to blame for making her a revolutionary, anyway. Doesn't mean you should ignore her, though."

"Yeah, just give me time."

"Fine. I'll give it to you now because if you've noticed, you're starting to wake up."

As she said this, the tanks began to go foggy, as if they were frosting over. "Don't worry, though, I'll be seeing you again sometime."

But I still know so little about you and Reeves! Please, I want to talk. You're wonderful.

And as she blew me a kiss good-bye, the tanks exploded into a rush of water around her before I jerked awake, remembering everything.

FIVE

IF MY life were a movie, I would have shot up straight in bed and screamed, "Holy crap!"

I would have begun writing everything down and tried to tell my friends.

But my life wasn't a movie, so instead I stared at the ceiling with eyes wide open in more ways than one. A life with as many complications as *The Twilight Zone* just got that much more confusing.

It was over a week until the next time I saw Ashlinn in my dreams. That time was mostly spent either in a garden or in ballet slippers, easy ways to occupy my body as my mind wandered back to the girl of my dreams and I pretended I wasn't lonely. I finally finished choreographing all ninety seconds of my dance, though.

Once I flooded a pot when trying to water some marigolds because I was thinking of how much higher in pitch her giggle was from her usual low voice. Another instance found me stuck in a split staring at my own reflection for God knows how long, dwelling on when she called our second meeting a date. Perhaps I shouldn't have been so fearful of telling her my sexuality. It almost seemed as if she felt the same way I did. Well, apart from the wariness in regard to a lot of things I had yet to explore and didn't feel the urge to. That whole "sexuality isn't set in stone" speech was nice, but I had to be a lesbian. I was sitting around wishing to hold the hand of someone who was definitely female.

A relationship was something I never had or particularly wanted before this, but she almost seemed worth giving it a try. Whenever I made up my mind to tell her how I was beginning to feel, there'd be a few minutes of brave bliss before the crushing realization that we could only be together in my sleep. How does one go about proposing a relationship with someone they only see in their subconscious?

Some nights, like after my weekly visit with Dad, I found myself sleepless. That would be angering enough on its own, but having blown an opportunity to have maybe seen her made it so much worse. Waking each morning trying to remember a dream that didn't happen was starting to drive me even more insane than before.

When Ashlinn finally visited me again, the relief was unfathomable. I had just started to worry I would never see her again, which was unfair considering how I had just worked out my feelings for the girl. Soon I probably would have decided the whole affair was a product of my imagination.

I had fallen asleep beneath my sheets, flat on my back, and the next thing I knew the ceiling above me became far more expansive and my bedroom fan vanished. A hotel room bed was beneath me now, one I had slept in as a child. Sitting up revealed a suite my family stayed in many years ago, except it was warped and twisted in a surreal manner. The walls were a violent shade of yellow and billowing like sails. A door clicked open, then slammed shut, and around the corner came Ashlinn in her cape, its billowing putting the walls to shame.

"Hello, heartbreaker," I sang happily. She gave me a casual salute in return, then perched herself on a cushioned plastic swivel chair that was placed diagonally from the bed. She began scanning through the little binder that would normally contain phone numbers and maps, then announced without any forewarning or trepidation, "I'm asexual."

"What?"

So many questions: What the hell is that? Why the hell are you telling me? Does this mean you're not interested?

But there was no time to ask; she was speaking again.

"You heard me. I thought it was only fair to even out the playing field. You accidentally opened up to me, so I'm just returning the favor."

She still hadn't looked up from the binder, seemingly engrossed in its contents.

"Okay, but what does that mean? Isn't asexual that plant reproduction thing we learn about in school?"

Evidently that wasn't the right thing to say, because she finally looked up and her face was unusually still.

"You honestly don't know?" she asked worriedly. I shook my head and wished I could burrow under the blankets more. The whole situation was making me feel like an idiot. She had been so good to me when I told her I was a lesbian, and I couldn't return the kindness.

"Well, I'm sorry to break it to you, but I'm not a plant. I just don't experience sexual attraction."

Oh. This was not how I expected our next meeting to start. All the hopes I had of us finding a way to make a relationship work began to fade away.

"I don't know if I understand," I admitted slowly.

"I was serious about researching other sexualities. Look this one up later."

Her tone was even, but there was a bit of a malicious undercurrent. Whether it was directed at herself or at me was up for grabs. Deciding not to dwell on whatever was making her angry and risk upsetting myself, I tried to change the subject. Better than addressing how uncharacteristically crushed I felt at the idea of her never wanting to be with me.

"We're in a hotel room. This is Baltimore, correct?"

Ah yes, stating the obvious always does so much to soothe someone's nerves.

"It's based on a room in Maryland, yes."

I got out of bed and walked over to the window where two layers of cheap curtains hid a striking view of the harbor. Moving them aside let in soft yellow light, which illuminated each building and sidewalk. It was morning. I registered Ashlinn's presence behind me moments before she began speaking.

"I did a good job on this one. It's beautiful." And nothing more truthful had ever been spoken. The sun was rising, casting the reflections of gleaming silver buildings onto the water.

"I always thought so. My parents, not so much. I remember this window from when we came on vacation," I told her, giving it a tap. "In the morning before Dad and Mother woke up, Reeves and I would slip behind the curtain and just watch the city come alive. We'd count the cabs lining up in front of the hotel and guess which color the next one to arrive would be."

As I told her this, a line of cabs pulled up on the street below us, and I looked back at her pointedly. She just laughed, holding up the binder from before, and said, "Let's order room service."

Looking through the menu revealed a long list of items one wouldn't find in a grocery store. Between the descriptions of pan-fried unicorn meat and well-juggled macaroon kebabs was simply the word smoothie in delicate cursive, and I took that to be the most harmless of everything on there.

Ashlinn told me to call the front desk and order, but I retorted that we were in a dream, so that really shouldn't be necessary. Lo and behold, without either of us lifting a phone, there was immediately a knock on the door and the food arrived. She ran over and opened the door, then took the tray from a well-dressed arm connected to someone I could not see and kicked it shut behind her before scurrying back.

I grabbed the swivel chair and a coffee table and pulled them toward the window so we could sit and look at the still water. As I sat on the coffee table, she handed me my smoothie, which was fluorescent orange and alarmingly glittery.

"What sort of drink is this?" I asked, holding it at arm's length. She reached for the straw and took a sip while it was still in my grasp, then shrugged.

"You know, it's really hard to manufacture tastes in dreams. I'd call this particular smoothie air flavored."

I tried it reluctantly and she was absolutely right. There was barely even a texture to the drink. Well, you can't be perfect at everything. We looked out the window and counted the cabs. She claimed the purple and blue ones while I called out the yellows, but we never really figured out who won. It felt so natural to sit there with her and make fun out of nothing.

There was a comfortable silence apart from the occasional shout of a color until something large and pink in the water caught my eye. I stood up, pushing back the coffee table with my legs, and got as close to the window as I could. It was a fleshy mass causing huge ripples with wriggling tentacles.

With a gasp I said, "Is that the—"

"Yes. That is the kraken. You said you expected him to appear in your dreams, did you not?"

I nodded slowly, watching as the creature ducked below the water, then erupted out again, which was a mind-blowing sight, but I was almost as taken aback by the fact she had remembered my offhand comment. My willpower was weakening, and I could feel myself falling for her even more, which just wasn't fair at this point. I barely even knew her, and yet she had more of me than most others, and she wasn't even solid. Or interested.

My curiosity was bottomless, but I didn't know how to go about learning everything I could about such a fascinating mystery. The only facts in my possession were her name, her sexuality, her job as a creator of dreams, and that she knew my brother. My brother who was in a coma.

"Shit," I whispered, "this is one fucked-up courtship."

Usually I left the swearing to Ellie, but this occasion seemed to merit such language.

"We haven't even gotten started yet," Ashlinn crooned back at me with a wink. I choked a bit.

"You know, you remind me of Ellie," I told her after regaining my composure.

"Not sure if I should be offended, considering it seems like you are currently avoiding her."

"Don't be. It's just you are both really open about things. Not afraid to speak. I always liked that about her."

"Should I be worried about competition?" Ashlinn asked me coyly.

"Not in the slightest. If anyone should be worried, it's me. What took you so long to see me again? Not holding your interest anymore?"

If the world were kind, that would have come off as joking.

"Quite the opposite, actually. Has it been a long time? It's always so hard for me to tell. I haven't done much since we last met. Saw Reeves, made a few people happy. The usual."

"How is Reeves? Did you tell him about Dad?"

She nodded, her eyes not quite meeting mine. "Yeah. He took it well enough, and I think he might have already had a feeling something else was wrong. There were tears, but if anyone can power on, it's that boy."

"Well, I'm glad he handled it better than I did."

She took my hand for a second and squeezed it. "I think you're both doing great. He really loves you, you know."

"I think I actually do. And I really love him." *And maybe you too.*

If it wasn't completely ridiculous, I could almost see myself starting to get jealous of Reeves. He got to see her all the time while I was left to pine away. It was still difficult to believe she was visiting him, and I was almost tempted to ask if she could bring me along next time. I owed my brother a carnation, some comfort, and a few stories. Before I could make any regrettable decisions, though, the dream began to evaporate around me, and I realized the morning was due. If only there was a way I could just remain asleep.

"Try not to take so long next time," I told her, and she waved as I was sucked away from her world.

Upon waking I rolled over and grabbed my cell phone to immediately begin researching asexuality. This time I remembered everything about the dream, and the details weren't escaping me like they usually did. I could recall her request vividly and had every intention of figuring out as much about her as possible. It was quiet, meaning Mother was already at work, so I had all day.

Definitions, pride parades, and a dating website popped up on page one of the search engine, but all the information about this sexuality seemed vast and varying. Not desiring sex was something I could grasp amazingly well, but some websites said asexual people would still engage in such activities anyway while others found that highly unlikely. One blog specifically stated to not make jokes about science class, and that didn't make me feel too hot. Eventually I ended up watching a documentary on asexuals in relationships.

Propping my tiny little screen on the bedside table, I turned the volume all the way up and grabbed some paper. My intention was to take notes on the subject as if it were an experiment, but about ten minutes in, I abandoned my notes as I had a crisis. There was a list of ways people could show affection without sex (massages, bathing, cuddles etc.) and it all sounded like more than I could ever hope for. There was an interview with one woman speaking about how she saw the beauty in others but never thought to apply the word "sexy" to any of them, and she wasn't ashamed when she spoke of her dislike of making out.

Oh my God, that's me.

So much of what they were saying was applying to me that I had to pause the movie and think for a bit. It seemed unfair to have to deal with more than one sexuality crisis in the span of high school.

Holy crap, could I be asexual?

For something I hadn't even known existed before that day, it was making a big change in my view of the world. Maybe I wouldn't ever be obligated to have sex with another person in order to make them stay with me. The thought was freeing: I wouldn't have to pretend. It was just a matter of finding someone else who understood.

And Ashlinn is this way too.

Except it was scary. Truly, skin crawlingly scary. Things were unlikely to work out with the voyeur to dreams; I wasn't so naive to believe otherwise. And then what? I could end up alone forever. Unloved and isolated. That wasn't the life I wanted to lead.

This wasn't the sexuality I wanted to have.

The documentary ended, and I felt increasingly pessimistic, then grabbed my phone and wandered downstairs to track down some late breakfast/early lunch. It was something healthy that I didn't taste, too busy examining my desires. Would Ashlinn consider a relationship with someone like me? It seemed impossible. There's no way such a thing could end well. Still, my mind continued to dwell on the prospect. I wanted to see her laugh so hard tears came to her eyes, to be close to her, to do the things the documentary had spoken of. Hell, I would have given an arm just for the ability to text her at that point. There was a sliver of hope, and it was more than what I'd had in the past several months.

After lunch I put on a leotard and practiced my dance. The choreography was finished, which was good, considering the audition was only one day away. Now it was just a matter of making it absolutely perfect. Those ninety seconds would dictate the course of my entire life. Every structured move that afternoon seemed to have Ashlinn's graceful gait injected into it, and I allowed her memory to inspire each pirouette. I was just about to take a break to get some water when my cell phone rang. I jogged up the stairs to where it was vibrating angrily on the kitchen table and answered, not even bothering to check who was on the other end.

"Hello," I wheezed, although it sounded more like a question in my breathless, postdance state.

"I have bad news."

It was Mother. Any bad news of hers was generally apocalyptic considering the last time I had heard those words, they were in the context of Reeves not coming out of his coma.

"What?" I asked, trying to hide the fear that had settled in my stomach.

"I have to go up to Edison. For three days." She worked her way through the words like she was walking a tightrope.

No. No. No.

"What about my auditions? They're tomorrow."

She sighed.

"I have no way out of this job. It's really important. Can't you schedule a different date?"

"Not this summer! I picked the latest one possible to have more time to choreograph."

And also so I wouldn't have to dance for an audience the month my father died.

I was on the verge of hyperventilating and had fallen to my knees on the kitchen floor. I closed my eyes and pressed my forehead to a cabinet.

"Calm down. I'm sorry. I'm so sorry."

Regret was beginning to seep into her voice, but there was no solace in that. Did she honestly think saying "calm down" would do anything?

"It's okay," I gasped, not meaning it for one second, and hung up not knowing if I'd be able to take it if the conversation had continued. I slid the phone across the tile floor, not caring where it ended up and didn't even try to steady myself. My whole future as a dancer seemed to be crumbling before me and all I could picture were worst-case scenarios. Instead of trying to figure out another way to get into the city or work on a backup plan, I just became hollow.

Ashlinn would help. Why wasn't there a way to speak to her like a normal teenager? My cell phone could have redeemed itself a bit if it worked as a way of communicating with her, but apparently there were no mobile phones in dreams. She was the only person who could offer any comfort, and she wasn't around. Fine. I could seek it in a more medicinal way, one that might end up getting me to her in the process. It was nearing the evening, and there was no time like the present.

Sleep would help. The thoughts in my head were as shattered as my dreams, but I knew that much. Images of my comatose brother and Dad's grave rolled through my head like a sick slideshow between thoughts of a future without pointe shoes. In that haze of despair, I found my way to the upstairs bathroom and its drug cabinet. White bottles beckoned and I shook them like morbid maracas, looking for one that was full enough that no one would notice if a few went missing. Codeine fit the bill, and its label revealed the contents could cause dizziness, shortness of breath, and light-headedness.

Like I didn't already have those.

I swallowed several down dry, ignoring the faucet in front of me.

Six

I REMEMBER feeling ashamed of the fact I wasn't ashamed of the act itself. I stumbled into my room, closed the shades against the fading twilight, and burrowed under my sheets to build a cocoon of darkness. Soon sleep would envelop me in a cloud of drug-induced serenity and I was finally calm.

This calmness extended into the dream. I was back at the start, where Ashlinn had first visited me, with sand beneath my feet and the ocean meeting the shore to my left. This time the fog was cleared away, and everything was placid and serene. Instead of having a gray atmosphere, lavender and pink skies spread out over the expansive blue ocean, and I almost forgot to be upset.

Almost.

Ashlinn's melodious voice came from behind me.

"Hello, Lovergirl."

"Hi," I responded, hoping this being a dream would prevent my voice from being too croaky. Something about my demeanor must have given my emotions away, though, because she grabbed my hands, worried.

"What's wrong? You can't be sad."

And I fell apart. There went the calm.

"I have nothing left. My family is gone and so is my future. You know the audition I have tomorrow? Mother can't drive me anymore. That school was my only way to escape from this town. I always hoped I could be something more than those other dancers, all the ones who thought they were gonna make it but gave up. It isn't freaking fair."

Ashlinn looked stonelike.

"Find another way to the audition." She sounded completely sure of herself.

"There isn't another way. What am I going to do, hijack a car I'd be too scared to drive? Ask Ellie? Or do you recommend I hitchhike and end up filleted in a ditch somewhere?"

"Personally I was hoping for something less violent. This isn't like you; stop giving up. Don't make me come out there and drag you to New York myself."

I lifted an eyebrow at her and scoffed.

"Now you're just being cruel. Losing everything I had ever hoped for is one thing. Having you dangle something impossible in front of me really sweetens the cake." I felt cruel but not wrong.

The water lapping onto the shore was discontinuous, and the waves kept pausing for irregular lengths of time, frozen in the air. Ashlinn had begun walking toward them and away from me, but that didn't stop me from hearing her when she said, "Reeves will be ever so disappointed."

"Don't you dare bring him into this!" I shouted. "I will not be manipulated. He does not need to know."

So much for her helping me. I was better off awake and miserable than asleep and patronized.

"Like how he doesn't need to know your mother is completely vacant now? I'm keeping that secret because you wanted me to, and I care about you. A lot. But he's my friend and deserves honesty."

"Says the girl who leaves me in the dark. I know practically nothing about you, but I want to know everything. There is no reason for you to be so mysterious." It didn't feel like a confession at the time.

She stopped her journey to where the water met the sand and, with her back still toward me, murmured, "You know nothing," in a tone so low it hardly met my ears.

"I know that you can hurt. That cape isn't body armor. When I heard all the work I put into this audition was pointless, the first thing I thought about was how you would know what to say to make it better."

"Sorry to ruin your illusions. I'll go now."

"This was so not worth taking all that codeine for."

I hadn't intended for her to hear my last statement. It was whispered under my breath, but her body noticeably seized up, and her head snapped back around.

"What did you just say?" she asked thunderously, stalking back to where I stood.

As if I was trying to prove some grand point, I proudly announced, "I was so damn pissed and eager to see you that I took some pills. Now look at what I get."

I held out my arms and tried to sound sure of myself, but the facade was slipping and she could definitely tell.

Ashlinn was face-to-face with me. Her furious eyes might as well have been burning holes in my flesh.

"Right, I'm ending this," she rumbled, and suddenly the landscape melted away into a dismal off-white.

The world around me flickered like a scene from a horror film, yet there was nothing to see in the moments of light. Thankfully, this hell lasted only moments, and the next thing I knew I was awake in bed, gasping.

My heaves quickly transitioned into screams when I registered another presence in bed with me. I scooted up against the wall and started flinging my hand wildly toward the bedside table to find a weapon, shrieking the entire time. When I finally had a flashlight in hand, I realized the intruder on the other side of my mattress wasn't a stranger at all.

It was Ashlinn.

"Holy crap!" I exclaimed, throwing myself even closer to the wall. It was a wonder I even recognized her, considering she didn't appear to have any clothing on, not that I could see any detail in the darkness. It was the first time I had ever seen her hair, a fact I wish I had been more ready to appreciate at the time. She looked at me with eyes that could have melted titanium.

"How many pills did you take?" she shouted as a hello, uncaring of her nakedness.

I wanted to answer, but the whole situation was so shocking I could do little more than stutter and stare as my brain attempted to come back online. Her voice hit me like lightening. I never realized how hazy dreams were until the crispness of her tone met my ears in reality. The revelation could be likened to the discovery of Mozart.

"Answer me. How many pills did you take?" Her distress was getting through, and I was finally able to stammer out an answer.

"Not too many. I'm not about to OD or anything."

"You better be right. Would you mind getting me some clothes?"

She was gazing down at my green sheets as if they held an explanation for her nudity. My mouth was complying in about the same fashion as my arms. Both were just hanging there unable to address the situation. She turned her eyes up toward me and stared heatedly until my brain began to work again.

"Yeah… um, I'll just grab you a robe."

I tumbled off the bed and toward my closet, feeling my way in the dark. This couldn't be real; there was no way. A creator of dreams was sitting in my bed, with skin and hair and an angry demeanor. Trying not to dwell on the insanity of the situation, I focused on the task at hand and began pushing aside the parade of sundresses behind my closet doors until I saw a pink terrycloth robe, which I presented to her from the side of the bed. Tears were starting to build up in my eyes.

She didn't thank me, and I made a show of turning around as she got dressed. After putting on my robe—*the color's all wrong; she doesn't wear pink, she wears midnights*—she inched over to where I stood and grabbed my arm to pull me back onto the bed. The contact was far too solid, and I convulsed a bit. She was warm and real, and I was hungry for more proof of her existence but was too scared to seek it. Our legs were dangling over the edge like when we sat together on the stage.

There was very little holding me together at that point. When she looked over at me with her still expression and said "Hello" so gently the words were hardly more than air, I began sobbing instantly. Thankfully, there was no hyperventilation as was my normal routine. This situation overwhelmed me, and my life was getting to be too much. She squeaked worriedly when the tears started falling and shimmied closer, grabbing my head and leaning it onto her shoulder.

I was chanting "you're real" over and over, which earned me a mouthful of bathrobe. It smelled of my detergent, but beneath that was the scent of rainy summer evenings. Her shoulder moved slightly with every breath, and I counted each one.

When I finished this well-earned emotional breakdown and gazed up at her, I must have looked like an absolute crime scene, but there was a sort of suppressed wonder in her eyes.

"Sorry about that."

"I had no idea my appearance would affect you like that. Not that you don't deserve it. I am absolutely furious with you."

"Understood. Stay pissed at me, but stay real. I can't believe I can actually touch you. Can I please touch you?" I reached out to stroke her arm but waited until I felt her give an almost imperceptible nod before laying my hand on her.

"How is any of this possible?"

"You should know by now that things from the world of my creation can easily enter yours. Look at the carnation drying up over there."

There was no need to lift my head and look at Reeves's flower to know it still sat on my bedside table.

"I hadn't ever allowed myself to exit before, but it wasn't difficult. Although I must admit I hadn't been expecting my clothes to vanish, not that you gave me enough time to expect anything."

"Why didn't your clothes come along?"

"They were created from whispers of creativity and illusions. Such fabric isn't exactly compatible with the waking world, or at least that's what I'm assuming."

"Great. Making clothes out of ideas. I may need a bit of time to process that on top of everything else. If you've always had the power to turn real, why didn't you do it sooner? I can't believe you're here. It's the most wonderful thing that could've happened."

A furious spark returned to her eyes, and she nudged me off her shoulder so we were level with each other. She moved farther back onto the bed and crossed her legs, so I mirrored her position and prepared myself for what was coming. It didn't seem like it would be pretty. Ashlinn took a breath.

"This isn't a reward, so please don't treat it like one. It's absolutely morbid. It's sick. You're throwing your life away, and it just isn't worth it. Are you insane? You could die. Then we'd never see one another again. How idiotic could you possibly be? Pills?" Her tone gradually got louder and darker as she progressed through this speech, and by the end she was seething. I reached over to her again, but she batted my hand away.

"I changed my mind. Don't touch me. This isn't an accolade, me being here. This is just me getting rid of ways you can hurt yourself and making sure you don't do it again."

I heard her words but wasn't paying as much attention as I should have. Sitting across from her offered me a fabulous view of her hair even in the dark. It was remarkably short and black with curls that stood out straight from her head. She noticed my distraction.

"You aren't even paying attention. Do you want to end up dead? Or like your brother?"

There was no reason for Reeves to be brought into this. Instead of going off on that, though, I decided just to tell the truth.

"I'm so happy you're here. You're real, and I'm looking at you and your hair with actual eyes."

She jumped off the bed.

"No, no, no. You can't be happy right now. I need you to regret your stupid decisions. Which way is your bathroom? I'm assuming that's where the drugs are."

I just stared down at the bed instead of answering.

"Fine. I'll find them myself. It shouldn't be too difficult."

Ashlinn walked out the door and I was alone again. No way that would last for long.

I leapt off the bed and began pursuing her before my brain could catch up. She was in the small bathroom across the hall, her face illuminated by strips of moonlight coming through the window's blinds. She had my small garbage bin in one hand

and was calmly chucking everything that came in a bottle and wasn't toothpaste or hair product into it. Disdain was evident on her face.

"Please stop," I said meekly, wrapping my arms around myself. She just glared and tossed a bottle of liquid Tylenol. "I promise not to do it again. Now that you're actually here, I won't need to." My voice was hopeful, but at this comment she dropped the portable pharmacy she was assembling and turned to me angrily.

"No. Self-destruction isn't cute. It isn't romantic."

"Oh, like you know anything about romance," I blurted, throwing my hands into the air. "You're freaking asexual; you probably know as much about romance as I do. I wasn't even sure you were real up until today and now you're teaching me about love. That's just brilliant."

The second those snarky words left my lips, I instantly regretted them. Defensiveness had gotten the best of me. It was unfair to use her sexuality against her, especially considering I might share it. Still, there was no retracting my statement, and I let it hang between us.

I'm almost tempted to say her expression was hurt, but there was too much fury to be sure.

"Have I ever said that I can't fall in love? That I am incapable of romance?"

"No," I stuttered back, ashamed.

"You didn't research it, did you?"

"Actually I did, and figuring out that I'm probably asexual too really didn't help matters. I don't want to be alone forever. I want to be loved."

God, please don't let me cry again.

Her expression was indescribable. She was enraged to begin with, so that emotion was expounded upon, but many others were at play as well. Now there were even more mistakes on my repertoire of regret. Her eyes were going glassy, but I would almost be tempted to say she seemed… proud.

"I'm so sorry," I gasped out, "for everything. For the pills. My words."

"I figured you would be."

"I just really hate being alone. I was so upset, and I'm really confused right now."

My tears fell like the tides, and there was no stopping them as my eyes blurred. Ashlinn finally softened and pulled me into a hug so I could rest my chin on her shoulder and thoroughly soak the bathrobe.

"I hate being alone too," she told me, "but I can't let you hurt yourself. Not for me. It just isn't worth it. Look, I promise to try and help you work out the asexuality, because it really isn't bad, if you promise to take care of yourself."

I nodded as best I could in my position and choked out a "Yes, of course." I was wary, but now she wouldn't leave immediately. I had an idea and figured it was time to grow some courage and voice it.

"Will you stay for a while? My mother is away for three days, and even when she does come back, I'm sure we'll be able to figure something out."

She seemed to mull this over, but her arms anchored me in place the whole time so I didn't become anxious.

"I'll stay for a bit. Someone's got to find a way to get you to that audition, anyway."

Elation is a troublesome thing. Impossible to describe but always explosive when felt. Of course I didn't actually believe what she said about the auditions. It was an impossibility, but instead of being saddened at her bringing it up, I just held her tighter. We stood there in each other's arms against the bathroom wall for a time, and soon the moonbeams would be replaced with morning sun.

"Come on," I told her, finally stepping back, "let me make you some tea. We can talk downstairs." I led her to the first floor, her hand in mine, the drugs abandoned forever on the floor.

SEVEN

NOT WANTING to lie in bed endlessly in the middle of the night had made me adept at the brewing of loose teas. For the past several months, I crept downstairs when the nightmares got too bad and distracted myself with warm beverages. Therefore, my actions were habitual and I didn't need to pay attention to my hands when making it for Ashlinn. The scent of vanilla wafted from the tin of tea leaves and permeated the air, adding another layer of calm to the situation, and I almost started wondering if I were dreaming again.

Looking across the kitchen at Ashlinn obliterated that thought, though. It was the first time I'd ever seen her in somewhat adequate lighting, and I couldn't stop staring, which was a good alternative to watching the tea. Her hair was barely darker than her skin, and its shortness just made her face's pointed structure even more apparent. Sharp angles dictated her whole bone structure, with prominent collarbones and knees.

She is a real girl breathing air in my kitchen with her bare feet on my tile floor and her arms in my robe's sleeves.

The kettle began whistling weakly, and before the sound could become piercing, I removed it from the heat and poured the water into a ceramic pot with the tea leaves inside. I then carried it out into the dining room and yelled behind me that she should grab some spoons and cups. Judging by the opening and shutting of cabinets, she figured out where everything was.

I poured the tea without looking at her, then stirred in one spoonful of sugar each. After closing my eyes for a few seconds to smell the tea and regroup, I looked up and asked, "Why did you never tell me this was a possibility?"

She just shrugged as she grabbed her china cup.

"Didn't want to get either of our hopes up, I suppose. I'm sure I would have told you eventually. It's not like I expected to take human form today."

"So you are human? You sleep and have lungs and everything?"

"This body is built in the same fashion as yours. I'm assuming it will tire." She paused to take a sip. "I don't recall ever having slept before, so that will be different. Speaking of things I've never done, this tea is remarkable."

It was actually too strong, as usual, but I grinned into my cup.

"You've never had tea before?"

"Well, I've never eaten or drunk anything real. Never had the need to. There are many things I've never felt the need to do, actually."

She was staring at me pointedly, not even trying to disguise what she was talking about.

"Right," I sighed, "I'll say it. I don't get this whole asexuality thing, and I'm absolutely petrified because a lot of what I've found out about it seems to apply to me."

"Like?" she asked when it became obvious I wouldn't continue talking without coercion.

"Cuddling without sex. Intimacy without, ya know, orgasms. That all sounds really great. I mean, I've never looked at someone and thought 'Wow that's a person I want to do the deed with' like everyone else seems to. I'd fake it in front of Ellie and all that and just assume I'd grow to like it one day, or that I was just a freak. And now apparently it's actually a sexuality. But...." I trailed off as Ashlinn nodded for me to continue. "Everyone else goes on about how great all that is, the kissing and the humping and all that jazz. How do I know I'm not missing out? That maybe I actually would like it? It's gotta be pretty great for so much of everyone's lives to revolve around the pursuit of sex."

"That's something you're going to have to find out yourself. You can still do those things and be asexual. It's the lack of sexual attraction, not celibacy. I'm actually fond of kissing as long as the other person's tongue doesn't find its way into my mouth. It feels nice."

I tried not to be jealous, but there was a spark of resentment over who she had been locking lips with in the past, even if I had no reason.

"Why did you kiss these people if you weren't sexually attracted to them?"

She winked at me. "Curiosity. And also because being a maker of good dreams has caused me to create my fair share of sex scenes. Honestly, though, I see it as more romantic than anything."

I screwed up my courage and looked her in the eyes.

"Would you kiss me?"

She refused to lose my gaze and didn't even pause, but set her teacup down on the table. "Depends why you want me to."

I could have said it was because she was the most marvelous person I had ever met and I wanted to share this with her, that I didn't think this was what I wanted, but she was someone I felt safe figuring that out with.

Instead I just said, "Curiosity." I felt like an idiot, and an uncomfortable one at that.

Still, she got out of her chair and walked over to where I sat. She cupped my face in her hands and looked into my eyes, assessing and, seemingly content with what she found there, knelt down and tilted my face toward her. Then we kissed.

The second her lips met mine a million dreams began to flicker before my still-open eyes. Futures I wanted us to have swirled through my brain as we stayed locked together. It was a short kiss, and rather chaste. When she pulled back, I didn't know what to think.

Actually, I did. I just didn't want to accept it.

Because that was something I never wanted to do again.

"Okay, I may have never been kissed before, but I'm pretty sure something about that wasn't natural. I saw visions."

She bit her lip. "I figured that might happen. I should have warned you. I am an embodiment of dreaming, so some of that seeped into you in our connection. Tell me the truth, though, did you like it? I'm not gonna be offended either way. I can deal with a life without kisses."

I toyed with the idea of lying to her. She said kissing was enjoyable for her, but the sincerity in those eyes as she knelt before me compelled me to be honest.

Also the fact that she implied she wanted a life with me.

"I'm not sure I ever need to do it again. It wasn't bad, just not really my cup of tea." And that was the truth. I'd had my first kiss, but it just seemed to be *there*, a memory holding weight, but more uncomfortable than enjoyable.

She grinned at my answer, obviously thrilled that I was being honest.

"We don't have to do that again. I hope it was helpful in the reanalysis of your sexuality."

"Among other things." I looked down at her before me, trying to read whatever played across her face. "You did just kiss me. Doesn't that mean something?"

"Only if you want it to."

She stood up and walked back to sit on the other side of the table and resumed sipping her tea.

"I don't think I've ever wanted any 'something' more if you're implying we can be in an actual relationship," I told her.

Ashlinn's grin was infectious, and I didn't remember ever having felt this happy in the past year without guilt.

"You need to stop being so charming," Ashlinn said, and I could hear the smile in her voice. "I'm not supposed to be rewarding you with this, and I keep forgetting to be upset."

"I'm not going to complain."

We drank in a silence that buzzed with elation. I had a girlfriend. If the day kept on at this pace, I'd probably end up queen of some European country by midnight. It seemed like something to talk about, but there weren't any words. When she did speak again, I heard shame.

"Actually, I did mean to apologize. I can't blame you for all of this. You may have picked up the drugs, but it is a little bit my fault. I made you addicted to dreaming. I've spoken of Semira to you before, correct?" She took a break from this monologue to sip her tea, although it was still scalding, and I confirmed that she had told me of the other dream maker.

"I have selfishly been keeping her away from you. People need to have nightmares or else they'd be in a perpetual haze of wanting to get back to their dreams. I did that to you and I'm sorry."

My nodding probably seemed a bit ridiculous at that point, but I had no words for the situation. There's no universe where this could be construed as normal breakfast conversation, but I did my best to treat it as such. This explains why the nightly flashbacks all but vanished when Ashlinn first showed up. Funny, I hadn't really thought about it. It just seemed to fit in with the way my life had become.

"No worries. I quite liked not having night terrors. Don't suppose you could keep it up?"

"Absolutely not."

Her presence was definitely worth the nightmares. Or so I thought. What she did next made me temporarily consider rethinking that sentiment.

"Now that we've gotten that out of the way, you must know the drugs aren't the only reason I came here." Her eyes were locked on the cell phone where it lay on the tile floor. "Your auditions are today, correct?"

"Well, not anymore. Can't go, remember?"

I figured I had every right to sound bitter. She obviously didn't agree because she lunged toward my phone on the floor, grabbed it, and without wasting a second, sprinted to the staircase.

"What the hell are you doing?" I shouted, pursuing her as she took the steps two at a time. The robe was trailing behind her as she skidded into my bathroom and locked the door.

"Let me in! What's going on?"

Calm down. Maybe she was just calling in pizza or phoning the president or something less ridiculous than what it seemed like was going on.

I pulled pointlessly at the door handle. The beeping of buttons echoed from the bathroom, and then there was a short pause. Someone was certainly taking a while to pick up, not that anyone could blame them so early in the morning. I turned my back to the door and slid down, throwing my head against it, hoping the bang it produced was loud and guilt inducing. The conversation we had just been having didn't lead me to any pleasant assumptions regarding who was on the other end of that call and why.

Ashlinn began speaking, but not to me.

"Hello, Ellie."

I swear, hell is empty.

There was a pause as she listened to a response, and I could hear my spirit chipping away in the silence. Good God.

"I'm her girlfriend, Ashlinn."

I was a cocktail of emotions, embarrassment mixing with horror, but hearing her use the term girlfriend did ease the negativity a little bit. There probably should have been more conversing before that proclamation was made, but for some reason, I wasn't bothered in the slightest. She had stated it so naturally, as if speaking of the weather or some other unchangeable fact.

"You need to drive her to New York today. Like, right now. You want her to be happy, and this will really help."

I was on my knees, lowering my head to the crack under the door to try and peek in, but to no avail.

"Hang that phone up right now," I shouted. There was no way this could work out. New York? With Ellie? Ashlinn was either insane or more out of touch with reality than I thought. She carried on the conversation as if she hadn't heard me, but the doors weren't that thick.

"Of course I'll come along."

There was another beep, and the door flung open—away from my face, thankfully—and I was eye level with her bare feet. I drew myself up as quickly as possible, and when we were face-to-face, I pulled her into a quick hug.

"That was for calling me your girlfriend," I told her, and she nodded accordingly with a sly smile, "but I'm not happy."

Her lips remained unchanging. She just shrugged and handed back the phone.

"You can be angry at me later. This evens us out a bit. Now go grab your dancing shoes. We're going to New York."

"I'm not ready. You can't be serious. We're not going to New York right now."

I made no move to act on her requests.

"You are ready. The choreography is finished. You always thought you were going today."

And I probably would have felt just as unprepared with Mother.

Having to do an audition I hadn't expected was one thing, forcing a neglected friend and a girl I was apparently dating to bring me was another.

How am I gonna tell Mother I actually went?

Seeing that I was unwilling to handle the situation, Ashlinn began taking matters into her own hands. She passed me and crossed the hall into my room, then flung open my closet to grab a sack-like over-the-shoulder bag. I followed her and watched as she pulled out a pair of sandals I never wore due to embarrassment over my feet and some sneakers. She grabbed a strapless sundress for herself and turned away modestly to put it on, taking her arms out of the sleeves but leaving the bathrobe on her shoulders as she stepped into the dress and pulled it up.

"Now find me your leotard and shoes."

My brain finally caught on, and I reached into the back of the closet to grab my outfit, tights and all.

"I need my résumé."

If we were going to do this, it had to be done properly. Mother was going to kill me if she figured out I went to the city alone with two teenagers, but she would find out only if I was accepted, which would undoubtedly ease the sting. I grabbed the folder I had prepared last week, grateful I hadn't lit it on fire or anything in my rage. As I packed this into a bag, making sure to grab my keys, Ashlinn walked over to the window, probably watching for Ellie's arrival.

"This isn't something you'll regret," she told me.

"I hope not. How am I going to explain you to Ellie?"

"Just tell her the truth. I'm sorry you believe I require such a massive explanation. You told me she thrives on social justice and defending minorities. I imagine finding out her friend is in an interracial same-sex relationship would make her life." She looked back at me over her shoulder with quirked lips.

"It's going to be so awkward. We barely speak anymore."

"And whose fault is that? She has a lot of happy memories with you. Maybe it's time to let her back in."

I opened my mouth to retort but realized there wasn't any counterargument. Shame was officially mixed into my cocktail of emotions. Thankfully, a crappy realization struck and replaced it with a different emotion.

"We're going to the city! I need money. Did you think this through at all?"

I ran over to my elephant-shaped bank, a relic from my youth, and opened it up. There was a twenty from my last birthday and some quarters.

"This is not enough. Mother will definitely notice if I pinch some cash from her too."

"Ellie likes you. I'm sure she'll chip in."

"If she remembered to bring money. It's not even eight in the morning yet. This is crazy."

Before I could fret any more and truly work myself into a nervous state, the doorbell began ringing out a discordant tune. I screamed in surprise.

"Our carriage awaits," said Ashlinn, ignoring my mania, and we walked downstairs with my bag.

It sounded as if Ellie was pressing the bell over and over again without pausing. When I meekly opened the door, she still had her hand on the button but quickly forgot about it in favor of pushing inside, saying "Where is she?" as her only greeting.

Ellie wore a cardigan—God knows why in early July—that had the words Cherry Bomb embroidered on the back in scarlet thread, the same shade as her lipstick. Judging by how her makeup was smeared on one side, she had slept in the stuff. It didn't take her a second to spot Ashlinn. You could easily pick that girl out in a crowd of millions, and Ellie ran over to pull her into a hug. Ashlinn reciprocated gently, giving me an unsure look over my friend's shoulder.

"Oh my God, I thought I was hearing things when you used the term girlfriend. Or that Victoria grew a new sense of humor and some deeper vocal chords."

She turned to glare at me, although I could tell there was no true fire in it.

"I can't believe you got a girlfriend and didn't tell me. I should have been the first to know. Hell, you should have told me before you even knew."

Like that worked out in the past.

"You actually are the first to know."

She lifted her eyebrows and seemed to mull these words over appreciatively for a few moments, nodding.

"Sorry, are you keeping this a secret or something? It's not like your mom would freak over you being a lesbian, right?"

I could see Ashlinn's eyes narrow at the word, and fearing she would feel the need to correct Ellie, I held up my hand and gave her a look to indicate we'd discuss the matter later. There was too much to deal with already, I didn't feel like explaining and defending asexuality on top of that. Not that I was sure if I could at that point. Ashlinn eased up a bit, and I gave Ellie an answer.

"My mother would probably be too shocked by my finding anyone to even notice their gender, but that hardly matters considering she isn't here. Which is why my *girlfriend*'—I put unnecessary emphasis on that word in particular, pleased with how it felt on my tongue—"thought it necessary to call you."

"I get it. I'm your backup. Don't worry, I'm not bitter. Just wish you could've given me a bit of a warning. We should be getting a move on now, though. What time is your audition?"

"Nine thirty."

Suddenly Ellie's cool demeanor slipped away, and she looked the most panicked out of us all. "Shit we really do gotta go. Shake a leg. I'm going to question you two about this the whole way there, so start preparing your stories."

She pushed the door open wider and made her way to The Hovercraft, leaving us in the house. Ashlinn gave me a hug so quick it barely happened.

"Sorry," she muttered, unrepentantly and with pride, and I repeated the word back to her. We walked out the door and toward my future, hand in hand, with my bag over my shoulder. An old Dodge had never looked so hopeful.

Ellie was already shouting out the window to hurry up. We both started to climb into the backseat when she took a break from her attempts at rushing.

"Not happening, your hot date sits in the front, or I'm not driving you. We have things to discuss, and I'm not in the mood to shout everything behind me."

Shrugging, Ashlinn closed the door and sat shotgun. I took my place in the back on the uncomfortable middle spot that wasn't really a seat, and we headed off. Ellie was drumming her fingers nervously on the wheel.

"What's freaking you out so much? I'm not even that worried about the time."

"It appears that I have neglected to mention how this particular piece of crap you are being taxied around in can't reach speeds higher than sixty-five miles an hour without giving up on life."

"What?" I screeched. "We'll never make it."

"You should have been quicker. First you call me at eight in the morning in the freaking summer after hiding the love of your life from me, and now I get abused for it. You're so damn lucky I woke up early today. With any luck we'll get there the moment your audition starts. It'll be great, like a scene from a movie. You can burst in victorious—hopefully there'll be two great big doors to fling open and march through—and kill the audition, then become a celebrity. It'll look great in the film adaptation of your life, I promise."

"Great, yeah," I muttered, staring out the front window. We weren't even out of town yet. Ellie rolled up the sleeves on her cardigan when we hit a red light, and reached over Ashlinn to get her sunglasses. Before returning her hands to the wheel, she poked her in the arm.

"Explain from the start. I want to know everything. You must be something special to have won this girl over," she said, nudging her head back to indicate I was the girl being referred to, as if it could be anyone else.

I was worried about what the response would be. In my mind any variation of the truth sounded like enough to get us delivered to the closest madhouse instead of the city, but Ashlinn performed yet another miracle.

"We met through family actually. I was a friend of her brother's. I always heard such wonderful things about Victoria and was pleased to learn they pale in comparison to the truth. After our initial meeting, I couldn't stop seeing her and just kept visiting. I'm not even sure if I was wanted."

"Well, I'd say you were, judging by the result," Ellie replied, laughing. "How long has this been going on for anyway? It seems like more than a two-day fling."

I piped up for this one.

"Oh she's been getting into my head for quite some time now."

Ashlinn choked back a snicker in the front seat and started looking out the side window.

"We started talking a bit before the end of the school year."

Ellie gasped. "You bastard. I've seen you since then, and you've said nothing."

She groped around next to her and grabbed a tube of lip gloss—the closest thing that could be utilized as a projectile—and lobbed it back at me. Thankfully, her eyes were on the road, so the aim was poor.

We were on the parkway at this point and no longer had to worry about children or small animals running out into the road in front of us. There was also a distinct lack of stop signs, which helped. The car had fallen into an amiable silence, although I suspected Ellie wanted desperately to ask more questions, and I willed the trees we passed to become blurrier. Instead, we puttered on at sixty as the other cars whizzed by. I imagined every other one held an applicant just like me except they'd be on time and confident. There was less than an hour left to get to the school.

The air began to turn heavy with anxiety. Every exhalation seemed like the ticking of a clock, and I didn't want this silence any longer.

"Can't you put on some music or something?" I asked.

Ellie reached over and turned on the CD player, which then proceeded to bless us with the discordant melodies of "Green Tambourine." Letting out a sigh of defeat, I face-planted into the seat to my right, the belt pulling uncomfortably in my lap.

"I can't do this audition."

"Of course you can. Stop being ridiculous," Ashlinn began. "You've wanted nothing more your entire life, and I shouldn't have to keep reminding you of this. The state of your feet should be reminder enough. If they don't like your dancing, they're fools."

"Fools with degrees and careers."

"You could stand there in one of your ballet positions just breathing and anyone with an ounce of sense would be enthralled. You're allowed to be nervous, but stop being discouraged. If we didn't think you could do it, we wouldn't be in this car right now. You were always going to audition. Now you've got a cheering section to make it that much better."

She delivered this little speech calmly, staring out the windshield the whole time except for at the end, when she turned around in the seat and looked at me where I lay flopped across the faux leather. Ellie seemed seconds away from taking her hands off the wheel to start slow clapping. She restrained herself to merely giving a low whistle of appreciation.

I righted myself, managing to kick the back of the driver's seat in the process of sitting up, while Ashlinn was still turned toward me. Her feelings for me seemed to be growing by the second, and I wondered if they were nearing mine for her. I wanted badly to say something profound, to worship the confidence she placed in me and try to will it to not be intimidating, but instead I just said "Thank you."

Ellie sensed that we were in an intimate moment and decided to have an outburst, probably to avoid feeling like the third wheel.

So, as Ashlinn gazed adoringly into my eyes and I looked lovingly into hers, Ellie blurted out "Got any entertaining kinks you wanna share?" Her tone was oddly nonchalant for the words and came without any preamble. Ashlinn wheezed like she might start choking.

"Ellie!"

"What? I'm trying to start a conversation. I can tell the girl my butter knife story."

I poked my head up between the seats.

"Oh no, not that one again."

Ashlinn seemed intrigued now.

"Butter knife story? How did you get from invasive questions to cutlery?"

Ellie grinned, preparing herself to relay one of her many ex-boyfriend tales, as I leaned back and tried to distract myself with the roof of her car. My desire to hear about anyone's sex life was less than zero.

"It's related, I promise. So once this boyfriend of mine had wanted to mix things up while we were having sexytimes. I, being a wonderful girlfriend, wanted to oblige him but, well, he had this thing for knives. I guess there's nothing wrong with that, but I wasn't too keen on hurting him and thought I'd end up doing damage. Also bloodstains and we were only fifteen. I had a brilliant idea, though. Once when we were getting all sexy together and I was lying across his chest, I pulled out a butter knife I had stashed in the bed and started running it over his abs. I tried to look all hot and everything, but when I looked up he seemed so confused. It must've seemed ridiculous, but the point is I tried. Okay, I've told you an embarrassing sex story. Spill yours."

This conversation was getting out of control. If this was my payment for getting to the audition, it wasn't worth it.

"You can't possibly be that embarrassed by it. You've told everyone with ears in a ten-mile radius."

She shushed me from the front seat, and Ashlinn spoke up, sounding much less uncomfortable and embarrassed than me. "Actually, I'm asexual."

Ellie let out a single laugh before realizing she wasn't joking.

"Wait, like the plant thing?"

"Nope. No. Definitely not," I interjected, recalling having said the same offensive thing. "It's a lack of sexual attraction."

Ellie looked at Ashlinn out of the corner of her eye.

"Then how are you guys in a relationship? I mean, masturbation's great, but I never took Victoria to be the type."

I covered my face with my hands and groaned. This was a disaster, a national tragedy.

"Goddammit, I'm asexual too," I blurted out before my brain could catch up to my lips.

"You mean you lied to me," Ellie responded, noticeably upset. "I thought you were a lesbian. You're in a gay relationship. Without sex aren't you guys just glorified friends?"

Ashlinn was silent and hadn't reacted to my accidental coming out, but now her voice was fiery as she turned to Ellie, who I feared was starting to get distracted from the road.

"Love is about more than sex. I know you know that. Look, I don't need you to approve or understand, but it'd be helpful if you tried. For Victoria's sake."

An expression of guilt colored Ellie's face after that particular jab. She just nodded. I had almost forgotten Ashlinn had been in her head as well and would know what strings to pull.

"I don't get it, and I can't say that I like it, but whatever charges your batteries. At least you don't have to worry about butter knives getting involved."

I had a few choice words for that, but we were running out of time to argue or apologize; the city neared.

Trees were gradually replaced by buildings, and I knew we would reach the Lincoln Tunnel soon. We had about twenty minutes, and I did my best to not think about that. On one side of the road was a library that looked as if it belonged in a fairy tale, while the other side housed a football field.

Before I knew it, we were in the tunnel. I gave a silent thank-you to the gods of E-ZPass for making me not have to waste my limited money on tolls.

Ashlinn looked enthralled as the yellow tiles whooshed past us, and her head was practically plastered to the side window. I told her to look out the front instead to get the very first available glimpse of the city.

As the light grew brighter in the tunnel, I began to feel half as excited as my girlfriend looked. I leaned forward between the seats again, intending to absorb everything about New York, but instead my attention was grabbed by Ashlinn, and she wouldn't let go.

Her eyes seemed to grow double their size. Without removing them from the sights bursting into view, she whispered, "It looks so different in reality," and it felt as if my heart were expanding. The buildings were a gray-scale rainbow with concrete carpets rolled out in front. Hot dog carts and falafel stands studded the streets in their grimy colors, and I could swear the smell of the rumbling subway's chain-smoker smog was already getting into the car.

Beautiful.

Ellie dragged me out of this reverie by snapping, "Yes, we're here. Now how the hell do we get to this school?"

I fumbled for my cell phone and plugged in the address as we crept down the road. There was a light before any major turns needed to be made, so I thankfully had enough time to let the GPS load. Ellie had definitely tensed up upon our entering the city, but I suppose the prospect of driving in New York could do that to a person.

"Keep straight for a few blocks. We're going to get onto Seventh Avenue at some point."

"Which you'll tell me. If you think there's any chance I can both look at signs and not hit pedestrians, you are mistaken."

The windows on the buildings around us were square jewels glistening with the reflected sun, and the people beneath them were weaving endlessly through each other like they were threads in a growing tapestry. Our speed no longer mattered because every car in the city was moving remarkably slow. I stared at the numbers on the dashboard's digital clock, attempting to slow them through sheer willpower. Ashlinn was still looking out the window with her hands up against the glass.

"Seventh Ave!" I screamed, realizing we were coming up close. Ellie veered to the left, and we managed to not miss the turn.

"Now we need to go all the way up to Fifty-Seventh."

That was only about ten blocks away. Ten of the shorter blocks. It was eleven minutes until the audition, and I tried to convince myself that a minute a block was a feasible concept.

Not that I was allowed much time to worry because Ashlinn suddenly shot up in her seat.

"You need to put on your leotard," she exclaimed, reaching for my bag and tossing it in my face. We really should have prepared for this better in advance. "You won't have any time to change once you get in."

I obliged, unbuckling my seat belt and stripping with a prayer that no one was looking in. My hair also had to be dealt with. There was no chance of making it. I did my best to hide in the area in front of the seat as I shimmied out of the pajamas I had on, grateful they were loose clothes, and stretched the tights on over my legs.

Ellie batted my foot away when it got dangerously close to the gearshift at one point, and soon I was pulling straps over my shoulders. Everyone seemed a bit too preoccupied to watch the world's most awkward reverse striptease.

A car behind us honked regardless of the fact there was a sign threatening fines against anyone who dared to violate the somewhat redundant noise ordinance, and Ashlinn gave out a shocked squeal. Ellie snorted at her reaction, which I responded to with a gentle whack on the arm as I twisted my hair with one hand into something that hopefully resembled a bun.

We crept down the road at a pace that only seemed to get slower as the audition time neared. Block after block passed in a numerical parade until we came to a stop. It was 9:29 a.m., and we weren't going anywhere. This only lasted the moments it took us to register our standing still.

"Dammit, girl, get out and run!" Ellie yelled, and before I could even think about it, Ashlinn reached into my open bag and shoved the shoes and paperwork into my hands. I opened the door.

EIGHT

THE SIDEWALK passed beneath me like a conveyor belt, and I noticed Ashlinn was running next to me with my bag flung over her shoulder. She reached out for my hand, and I grabbed it, after which she doubled her speed, dragging me along.

We ran straight through two crosswalks, praying that no cars would come barreling. The building, a great glass structure, stood at the end of the block, and I pointed at it with my free hand, trying to suppress the burn in my legs. It would only increase during the dancing, and there was no time to warm up.

Her hand in mine was the only force propelling us forward. Everyone else on the sidewalk melted into a blur as they jumped out of our way. She pulled me to a halt in front of the rotating doors and before I could be pushed into my future, I threw my arms around her and hugged her tightly. When we parted she aimed me in the direction of the building.

"You're already two minutes late. We'll have time for this later."

And before I could make her turn that statement into a promise, I found myself walking into the glass box of a lobby.

There was a long, white table with a sour woman sitting behind it who looked as if she may have been a dancer at some point as well. She beckoned me forward to sign in while chastising my lateness. Looking down at the paper revealed a long list of others who had made it before me, and I signed Victoria Lindy Dinham at the bottom of the section for dance majors. Glancing at the list showed me names that already sounded like they would fit in among proper dancers and actresses.

With a glare the lady pointed me toward the door to the audition room.

"We do not tolerate when students are tardy to class. How do you think showing up late to your audition will make you seem?" she snapped. "Now go on in."

My stomach felt as if it were turning in on itself. Before entering I slid on my shoes, which were still in hand, noting how torn the bottom of my stockings had become courtesy of the New York streets. I could feel the woman's continuing judgment at my delay as I tied up the ribbons, and gave her a small wave before heading in.

The room was uncomfortably big and mirrored on one side. I almost stopped dead upon seeing my reflection, complete with flushed cheeks and hair sticking out of the bun, but carried on. Opposite from where I entered sat another woman with a similar bearing to the first. She was behind an identical white table, although this one had a tripod-mounted video camera sitting on it. She was not smiling, but also not frowning. That was a start.

She gestured toward the empty space in front of her as a signal to begin, and I rattled off my slate. I could hear the tremor in my voice as I told her my name, hometown, and life goals. Then I handed her my phone, taking a moment to track down the music, and once it came pouring out of the speakers my body fell into the familiar moves of the dance.

The melody was so much louder in this room, as if the mirror was reflecting sound as well as light. It took a great deal of willpower to not be shaky and out of breath, still not fully recovered from the sprint to get there.

Ninety seconds.

All I needed was a minute and a half of perfection and nothing else; everything had built up to that since I was a five-year-old in a tutu. With an emptying breath, I rolled up onto my toes.

Every step I took was a prayer that this one woman watching would see something worthwhile. Having the music so loud was almost as extreme as when Ashlinn had had me dance without any at all. Unlike that instance of dancing for an audience of one, this time I was able to successfully transition from a chassé to a pirouette and not end up on my face. At least I had that going for me. My feet were crescent moons, arched in pink leather and cramping.

I tried to leave my mind blank of everything but the next move, even if that meant I had to focus on the pain, on the overexertion of my arms and legs. Ballet was pushing your body past what evolution meant for it to be capable of, to break the laws of nature in a quest for beauty. Dammit, I trained at East Coast ballet studios. Angry, retired, ex-Broadway dancers own every one and didn't give wiggle room. If I could do one thing, I could kill this audition.

After the music stopped, I held my position, trying to read the woman's expression the whole time. She wasn't looking up at me but down at some papers lying on the table. It made me worry if she had actually seen any of my performance or if she would just watch all the videos later. Without music the room was frighteningly quiet, and every breath sounded like windstorms. She finally looked up at me with a masklike expression that nothing could be inferred from. Something came over me in that moment, and I stared her in the eye.

"That was for my father."

As I grabbed my cell phone, she just nodded and gestured toward the door, telling me to meet with an admissions officer. I'd get my results in a month.

The admissions officer was a man named Neil, although boy was a better term; he barely looked older than me. His hair was modern, shaved on one side, and he had a smile that could only have come from years of living in an orthodontist's chair. My lingering nervousness dissipated slightly at his friendly demeanor, but I still felt uneasy. There was no way to know if my dancing had been good enough, and I had nothing left but to analyze my slipups for the next four weeks. Neil and I sat at the third white table I would become acquainted with that morning, and I was relieved to see a few other stragglers finishing up their interviews.

"So, how do you think you did?" he asked, leaning over the table. He sounded like someone trying desperately to seem more relatable and cool than he truly was.

"It probably wasn't the best audition in the world. I did show up late and sweaty. But I really put my everything into it."

I flashed him a smile straight out of any romantic comedy.

"That's what we like to hear."

He returned the smile, but I couldn't tell if it was condescending or not. He shuffled around some papers, and I twiddled my thumbs uncomfortably but tried to keep my eyes trained on him. Perhaps I was asserting dominance, or maybe just pretending I wasn't completely terrified.

"Why don't you tell me about some challenges you've faced so far in life."

Wow. They really hit you with the big questions early on. I had expected this to just be a conversation about financial aid and extracurriculars. Closing my eyes as if I were about to perform yet again, I took a deep breath and prepared to bare my soul. Anything to get out of suburbia.

"I can start with the fact that my father died a year ago in a car accident. He used to plant red flowers and bring me to all my dance lessons."

Neil began blandly apologizing for my loss, but I held up my hand and interrupted his pitying words. He didn't know me; how could any sentiments of his be more than a farce? If he spoke, the tears would begin. They needed proof I knew the show must go on.

"He would cut those red flowers and wrap them in newspapers to give me after performances. Other girls would get nice grocery-store bouquets but mine had been cared for from the start by my father. Like me. That same day, the one I lost him, my brother Reeves became comatose."

Neil was nodding. He must get to hear a fair share of sob stories on a daily basis when that's one of the interview questions. I ignored his movements and continued.

"And I've just kept dancing. I don't know if I've overcome these things, but the music never stopped, so neither did I. It's not like I have much else."

That was all I had to say, but it didn't feel like the right note to end on. Life was becoming less cynical. He was a bobble head and opened his mouth to begin asking the next question, when I interrupted yet again.

"Actually, that last bit's a lie. I have this dishy girlfriend now, and she is the best thing that has come out of all this shit."

My eyes widened in fear of having allowed the swear to slip out, but his cool-guy demeanor just seemed to brush it off.

"I'm very happy you have someone. That's important, especially when dealing with such tough circumstances."

He conducted the rest of the interview a bit more formally, not bringing up the first question again, and what remained was more or less what I had expected going in. Without seeming too desperate, I told of my need to get into this school and how I had zero desire to study abroad. I defended my lack of extracurriculars other than dance, and he let at least the last year slide. More than anything, it was like a conversation with an upperclassman I wanted badly to impress.

The interview ended around the time I had actually begun to compose myself. He walked me to the door where I displayed my impeccable manners by shaking his hand and thanking him. Then I went into the glass lobby where I stood in the corner and removed my pointe shoes. That drove home how much pain they had truly caused, and I cringed with my mouth wide open, probably to the amusement of the sour-faced woman sitting behind her table. On top of it all, I forgot to bring socks. This wasn't going to be a painless day. Still, I got them off and crossed through the lobby with torn tights and an upturned chin and found my way into the city. Now all that was left was to wait. It was almost a relief to have the matter in the hands of someone else.

The bustle of the streets nearly swept me along the second I hit the sidewalk, but I managed to flatten myself to the building and avoided being run over. I didn't have time to wonder where Ashlinn had gone before getting an armful of my girlfriend out of nowhere. I nearly had a heart attack when she flung herself around me, chanting "How did it go?" several times, blocking my attempts to actually tell her.

When she finally calmed down to the point where she was merely squeezing me like a black-haired boa constrictor, I answered.

"Shockingly okay, considering I felt the opposite of prepared."

I didn't have it in me to spoil her ecstatic mood with my doubts, and I succeeded, judging by the way she grinned. Looking over her shoulder as we hugged, I realized someone was missing.

"Where's Ellie?"

Her voice came from directly behind me.

"Here, just pretending to not be a third wheel as you get your little reunion over with. Jeez, you guys were only apart for what, twenty minutes? Thirty?" She didn't sound bitter, just joking. I let go of Ashlinn, and Ellie gave me a much shorter congratulatory hug.

"What did you do after we left?" I asked. "It's probably really bad that three teenage girls split up in New York City."

Ellie shrugged. "It's practically Disney World out here with the amount of tourists. I managed. There's a parking garage around the corner. A very overpriced one, I'll have you know. We can only stay a few hours. It was nice enough for me to drive you, but I don't plan on going broke from today. Anyway, I dropped off The Hovercraft and ran back here. Thankfully, your hot date was waiting outside or else I would have been texting you in the middle of the audition."

I realized they had spent the entire time I was dancing and interviewing for my life hanging out with little to do. Ashlinn could have said anything about how we truly met. Ellie didn't seem too traumatized, though, and I got no sense that she thought either of us was insane. My only prayer was that she had refrained from telling any more stories like the butter knife incident. God knows she had a lot saved up for such occasions. Most of the time I stayed sane by assuming she made them up. Even one of those tales would be preferable to her questioning asexuality, though.

"We gotta get a move on if you intend to do anything fun today. We don't have much time and I think we're getting in the way over here. How much money did you bring?"

Ellie was never one to mince words when asking questions. I reached into my bag, which was still flung over Ashlinn's shoulder. Seeing the normal clothes she had packed brought on a wave of uncertainty over standing in public in just a leotard, but I pushed those fears back one spot in line and found my change purse.

"About twenty bucks." I had hoped some more money would have magically winked into existence during the audition.

"That won't do much if we're going to eat today, and there's no way you're starving me. Okay, we'll just go to Rockefeller Center and Central Park. They're free, close, and we can't waste the day thinking of something to do. Come on."

Before she could leave us behind, I pulled out my sundress.

"I'm not going in ballet shoes and spandex."

She groaned. "Go change, and make it quick."

"Where do you propose I go? I'm not walking back in there, and I don't think the cops would approve of me stripping in the streets."

She popped a hand on her hip and looked at me over her sunglasses. "They should be grateful for the free show. Fine, duck into the next Starbucks we come across. There's about three on every block."

And with that she marched forward ahead of Ashlinn and me without even awaiting a response. We diligently followed. We reached the next Starbucks before we even came to an intersection, and it was so packed no one noticed when I ran in and out without buying.

With the pointe shoes already gone and my leotard following suit in mere seconds, I began peeling off the tights. That was a gift, even in the claustrophobic stall of the bathroom, and soon I was wearing an airy sundress and sneakers and was out in record time. Ellie resumed leading the way immediately.

We walked down the streets past stores I could hardly afford to look at, and homeless people camped out in front of them, asking me for money I could not give. At one point, Ashlinn nearly walked in front of a speeding taxi, not understanding what the red hand flashing on the opposite side of the crosswalk meant, and I grabbed her arm to stop her. Ellie was already across the street and smiled knowingly when I released Ashlinn's arm in order to hold her hand.

She said nothing, still awash with the marvels of the half-glittering city around us.

It reminded me of the graveyard more and more as we progressed toward Rockefeller Center. Some of New York was crumbling, empty of its original purpose, and forgotten, while the other half was well loved and glistening with shimmering statues and sausage stands.

We crossed the street and rejoined Ellie, and from this new vantage point saw the golden wealth and bursting fountains like a mirage among the steel structures. She began jogging toward this oasis and we followed, a pair of sundresses rippling in the wind.

The area was vast and filled with tourists snapping pictures. Together we headed to the low brick wall surrounding what would be an ice skating rink during the winter, but now just circled a small café from above. There wasn't an overabundance of customers, and many of the chairs were still in stacks, although some employees were beginning to place them around. Ashlinn put her arms on the ledge and her chin on top in order to watch, and I copied her posture, as did Ellie.

The area fell in the shadow of a magnificent statue of some god I couldn't name.

"That bastard must have done something really great to merit being golden," Ellie said, tilting her head in the direction of the figure.

"He really did. That's Prometheus. He kept humanity warm and in return is getting his liver pecked out by birds for all of eternity. The least you guys could do is give him a half-decent statue."

Ellie turned her head toward Ashlinn, looking surprised, if not taken aback, obviously not expecting her to be so knowledgeable on the topic.

NINE

WHO WOULD have thought that sentence and the ensuing diversion would have ended with us being kicked out of a jewelry store with Ellie wearing one less flip-flop?

"They deserved to have it tossed at them," she grumbled after I admonished her for attacking salespersons who didn't mean any harm.

"It's not like they were lying when they said we couldn't afford pearls. Have you seen the state of us? Everyone else in the place had a Versace suit."

If she heard me, she gave no sign of it.

"This is classist!" Ellie yelled over her shoulder in the general vicinity of the store we had just been escorted out of. I ignored her in favor of listening to Ashlinn, who pulled me down to whisper in my ear.

"You did say she was a bit of a revolutionary. I thought the dreams of world domination were exaggerated, but I'm starting to believe it."

"What a world that would be. We'd all have diamond necklaces and free tampons. Doesn't sound too bad, actually."

"She can get you whatever necklaces she wants as long as the rings are left to me. I saw you eyeing up those engagement rings. Never took you to be a platinum girl."

My ears were burning, and I could feel the blush pulsating red in my cheeks. Not meeting her eyes, I said, "It'd be hard not to be."

We shared a smile as Ellie glared, probably perturbed by the whispering. She was padding along beside us as we wandered slowly and without direction, only flopping with every other step. Just looking at her bare foot on the uncomfortable streets of New York made my inner WebMD throw up in protest.

"You're going to catch so many diseases that way. We have to get you some shoes."

"With what money?"

"Well, don't you have some left?"

She shook her head. "I still have to pay for parking, remember? I don't trust the rates posted, so none of my money is getting spent."

"Do you want to get tetanus?"

It was the first disease that popped into my mind, and I wasn't even sure if that was something one was likely to contract from city concrete, but she thought for a second. I could almost see her weighing the options, groaning.

"You're paying for half."

"Deal."

She didn't have to know the money was being removed from her already feeble lunch fund. Thankfully, being on an island-length tourist trap put us in close vicinity to a shady, doorless corner shop even after having just exited Louis Martin. There were carts of fifty-cent postcards on racks outside, the mildly pornographic ones pointed away from the street, and scarves draped from every shelf. The knickknacks were plastic, and I wouldn't have been surprised if the entire shop was a front for drug or weapons sales as there was a distinct absence of customers, even though it was the busy season.

Black flip-flops with hearts printed on them in a rainbow of colors dangled from a bar on the wall. Ellie grabbed a pair at the end without even checking the size, and walked the two feet it took to get across the store to toss them on the counter. Ashlinn was busy in the back, tapping bobbleheads and shaking every snow globe she could get her hands on. The cashier, a wrinkled and bearded man with stained clothes, rang up the purchase with an indifferent expression, then demanded eight dollars, which Ellie grumpily proffered four of while I dug out the rest.

Ignoring his offer of a bag or scissors, she tore the tag and plastic tie off on her own and slipped them on. The single shoe they replaced found its way into an overflowing garbage can.

After grabbing Ashlinn from where she was distracting herself, we headed out.

"We probably shouldn't be wandering too far from the parking garage," I said, realizing we were going in the opposite direction.

"But I wanted to go to Central Park and climb the rocks," Ellie whined insistently in my ear.

"How much time do we have left?"

She took out her phone and frowned at whatever she saw there.

"About an hour. It'll be enough time if we hurry up. Start jogging."

With that she was off toward the distant green. Block after block we trotted at a steady pace, and I lamented the soreness my legs would inevitably feel for days, not to mention the damage being added to my feet. Ashlinn was worse off than me, though, and it seemed like the only things preventing her lungs from giving out were the breaks at stoplights. If we were training for a marathon, it would be one with a horribly inconvenient dress code.

After a few blocks of sweating and sprinting, we crossed over to the entrance. It was framed by carriages on one side and fenced bushes on the other. Panting, Ashlinn asked, "How long did that take?"

"Ten minutes."

"We have forty left. I can work with that." She grabbed my hand and headed toward the boulders. "Show me the life I never led."

Ellie walked ahead of us on the smooth expanse of rocks, probably not wishing to stare at our perpetually linked hands and be reminded of her solitude. With hands in the pockets of her cardigan, she strolled along, appearing certain the boulders wouldn't dare make her stumble even as they started to turn ragged. If she did trip, her arms would not be available to brace the fall.

As the rocks began to grow higher, they also became more uneven, with crevices splitting them into geometric patterns. Wary of our clothing, I had Ashlinn climb ahead of me as I made sure no one could see up her sundress, then allowed her to help me keep my balance as I followed.

Ellie was up there waiting for us as we got to the highest part and looked down on a baseball field. "Walking around on rocks shouldn't be this entertaining," I said as we stood in a line, taking in the surroundings, from the park full of children to the rows of buildings standing like a deck of cards.

"They wouldn't have left them if someone didn't find it fun. Just think, they've lasted here since the Ice Age and we could tear them away with a bit of machinery in no time. The mammoths would be jealous. I don't know if anything can truly be permanent anymore."

I'd say Ellie was in a bit of a philosophical mood, but if she was, it had started with her exiting the womb.

Ashlinn's eyes hadn't left the playground the entire time we stood there. It wasn't much, but there were bridges and slides and a swing set.

"We can go if you want," I told her, and she began her descent immediately without even answering.

Climbing off the rocks was actually more difficult than going up. There were uneven ledges to jump between and small chasms and crannies to use as a steep staircase. I was forced to release her hand in order to cling to anything I could lay my fingers on.

When we finally hit solid ground, I said a silent prayer to whatever gods might be tuning in, thanking them for my not having lost any limbs. We also managed to not flash the children with our dresses, always a plus.

Ashlinn took no time to reclaim my hand as she skipped toward the swing set. One free swing was being eyed by a young boy, but I didn't point him out to her. I just hurried up and all but threw her into the seat.

"I'll push you. Hold your dress down."

Standing behind her, I grabbed the chains and pulled back, bringing her along, then pushed her shoulder blades. Her back beneath my hands was warm and slightly sweaty, another reminder that she truly was here. Ellie was on the slide, dragging her feet along the sides as she went down in an attempt to brace herself from plummeting straight into the wood chips. She waved at us and began climbing the ladder again, not ashamed to be the oldest person on the playground apart from parents. A few were shooting unfriendly looks at the three of us, but nothing could bring me to care.

Ashlinn was flying through the air, the dress blossoming beneath her hands with each swing. She was laughing as if she had never been happier, and if anything kept the adults from kicking us out, I'd say that was it. No one would ever want to prevent such melodious joy.

Ellie called to me from the bridge she was running across, now with a trail of small children chasing her, but I couldn't make out her words above the swing set's metallic creaking. When Ashlinn came rushing toward me again, I wrapped my arms around the swing to stop its motion and ended up getting dragged as the momentum continued. When I let go, she stumbled out as I kneeled behind the swing with scraped legs.

"Well, that wasn't the most elegant thing I've ever attempted."

There were red wood chips inlaid in my knees and hands now, and I began picking at them as Ashlinn squatted next to me, staring. Ellie was laughing at my expense even though she was a fair distance away, and it spurred me onto my feet and toward her.

"What did you say?" I yelled up from the ground.

"We've got ten minutes left. Then it's time to head toward the car. How much money do you have?"

"Sixteen dollars to spend."

"Awesome, you're buying us cashews."

On one of the sidewalks snaking through the park there was a rickety little cart with a faded red umbrella above it. A man scooped our nuts into three small wax-paper bags. It was a sad excuse for a lunch, but with the amount of cash we had left, I was grateful for it. Judging by the blissed-out expression on her face, Ashlinn was as well.

We plopped ourselves on a bench right on the edge of Central Park, and as in all situations, Ellie had a story for this one.

"Once my mom saw a pigeon in one of those things, right in the glass with the nuts. The man just shooed it out and continued selling them. Don't even think he was embarrassed that people saw."

"If you're trying to ruin my appetite with that nugget of info, I'm sorry to tell you it isn't going to work," I told her.

Ashlinn was watching the cars go by with intent, and the second a purple taxi passed, she smugly informed me that she was winning. I remembered us counting the cabs on our third date together and grinned like a lunatic.

"You have no chance of winning. We're in New York and my color was yellow."

I was scanning the streets for glimpses of the color and saw three canary yellow cars in a row. I jumped up to point them out so excitedly that I dropped some cashews. It would make a good dinner for the birds, at least. Ellie must have accepted that the whole thing was some sort of inside joke and just went on eating her nuts.

By the time we stopped, I had dozens of points while Ashlinn had spotted only two more purple cabs and no blue ones.

"As much as I hate to interrupt this truly riveting game of identifying colors, we really must start heading to the garage."

Ellie seemed disappointed, but her emotions were amplified tenfold in Ashlinn. It looked as if her heart was breaking, and I felt mine go along with it.

"Don't worry," I told her. "We'll come back."

I wasn't sure how true those words were, but it seemed like the right thing to say. Our journey back to the parking garage was tinged with the sadness of having to return to New Jersey. We didn't have to sprint as much and speed-walked like I had a tendency to do through the hallways of school. Hand in hand we headed to our way home. Thankfully, Ellie had enough money for the time we'd spent, and we were able to hit the road at midday when many were just arriving.

Both Ellie and Ashlinn were worn out from our little foray into the city, but it felt like I was only starting to wake up. We passed an old indie movie theater that looked like something hipsters would frequent with cans of Pabst Blue Ribbon in hand. A poster for *An American in Paris* was framed outside the door.

"Look, it's you," Ellie said when we got caught in traffic next to the building. She was gesturing at the image of Gene Kelly as he danced across the painted poster.

"I wish."

Ashlinn scoffed. "What does he have that you don't?"

If we were facing each other, I would have dumbly stared at the girl for a few seconds.

"That's Gene freaking Kelly. He has absolutely everything plus some. Are you telling me you've never seen *Singin' in the Rain*?" The thought was a blasphemous one. Ellie sighed in the front seat, probably remembering our elementary-school days when I spoke of little apart from movie musicals and old dancers. She had been subjected to several marathons, poor girl.

"I haven't seen most movies. That shouldn't really come as a surprise to you."

"I guess not. That settles it. We are going home, building a blanket fort, making a disgusting amount of popcorn, and watching this cinematic masterpiece."

"And I will be as far away as humanly possible," Ellie informed us before wishing Ashlinn luck.

The drive home was an easy one, and the air of nervousness from this morning had mostly melted away. No one brought up any controversial conversation topics. There was just excitement about all the time I'd be able to spend with Ashlinn. Waiting for the results of my audition would be hellish, but I imagined she'd find several ways to keep my mind off it.

It was the afternoon by the time The Hovercraft pulled up outside my house.

"I'm going to go take a six-hour-long shower and exfoliate. This whole slept-in then-citified look isn't really working for me. Hey," Ellie tacked on like an afterthought, although she probably had wanted to ask us all day, "would you two care to join me when I get my tattoo in three days?"

"Absolutely," Ashlinn exclaimed before I could have any say in the matter, and Ellie looked relieved as she told my girlfriend to "enjoy the excruciatingly long dance numbers."

The advice she offered me was different.

"Don't change for anyone, Victoria," she told me as if I were intending to. "Now get out of my car, you whatever-you-ares."

I unlocked the house with the key I was grateful to have remembered. It was different to be with Ashlinn in the living room with light. Everything had been calm and illuminated by the moon until it exploded into a trip to New York, but this felt average. It didn't seem like a situation she belonged in. This was real life. What if we ran out of things to talk about? Or if I lost whatever sparked her interest in me? I couldn't deal with a life consisting of the sound of forks against plates, like what I shared with Mother.

The cross-body bag got tossed next to my school one where it sat in the corner. I think she noticed my wariness as we stood facing each other right inside my entryway because, like the wonderful person she is, she just said "*Star Wars*."

"What?"

"*Star Wars*. You expected me to know about movies, and that's one I basically get the whole plot of. Siblings that kiss. Talking metal men. There's some crazy stuff going on in the films you guys watch."

It was absolutely absurd and completely gorgeous.

"Why that movie?"

"I've had to concoct a lot of dreams based on it."

That made sense. I grabbed her hands in mine and began swinging our arms, not for any reason other than that I could.

"I always pretended to hate that series growing up because my dad loved it more than most things. It was funny when he'd get angry over me insulting it."

"Very devious of you," she said, then stood on her tiptoes and leaned toward my face.

For a second it seemed like she was making to kiss me on the mouth, and all my limbs locked in place, confused, but instead her lips landed straight on the tip of my nose.

"Okay?" she questioned. "Sorry, I probably should have asked first."

"No, that was nice."

I didn't meet her eyes. A part of me was hoping I'd never get used to this, that her affection would amaze me every time.

"Well, I was promised a blanket fort and some popcorn. Shall we?"

She released my hands and looked at me as if awaiting directions. After regrouping for a few seconds, I sent her around to grab every blanket and pillow she could find on this floor, telling her to open closets and dismantle couches, while I began searching for popcorn in the cabinets.

As it popped she walked past the kitchen with two blankets balanced on her head and another dragging on the floor behind her like the train of a gown. There were so many pillows stacked up in her arms I don't know how she could see over them at all. Sheets were stuffed in randomly among everything else and looked like they were getting ready to tangle in her legs.

"At least if you trip, you have something soft to land on." I laughed, grabbing half of the pillows.

In an attempt to remove the blanket from her head, I just ended up pulling it over her eyes. She shook it off like a disgruntled puppy would, and I did my best not to look as endeared as I felt. A weak facade. I never claimed to be an actor, only a dancer.

She began her journey to the living room yet again and I followed. After dumping the beginnings of our cushiony cocoon, the microwave beeped and I ran back to get the popcorn.

"It's not much of a meal—"

"It's perfect. Do you realize how amazing that smells? Humans don't know how lucky they are."

Her wonder was completely unbridled and utterly contagious. The popcorn did smell nice, but honestly her appreciation of it made any other pleasantness pale in comparison. I placed the bowl far away on the floor and looked at the lump of blankets. We were going to need a game plan for how to go about arranging them into a fort.

"Ever had a sleepover before?" I asked while grabbing one side of a crocheted orange quilt. She grabbed the other end so we could pull it over the couch.

"My entire life is a sleepover. I have inadvertently 'slept over' at most everyone's house at one point or another."

"You know perfectly well that doesn't count. We're going to have a proper sleepover. The blanket-fort-movie combo is a good start. Next we're gonna need 'would you rather' and scary stories. By the end of the night, our bras will probably end up in the freezer."

Her eyes widened at the thought. We laid a blanket over the couch and stacked pillows on top in an attempt to anchor it.

"Are you sure you even know what happens at a sleepover? I've seen some crazy things in the minds of teenage girls, but frozen undergarments tend to stay out of it."

"I've seen lots of movies that have sleepovers in them, so close enough. And I spent a lot of time sleeping over at Ellie's back in middle school. We mainly just watched marathons of *Law & Order* in her basement."

I folded the other end of the quilt over a chair, and she mirrored that on her end. Then we draped blankets over the top so they covered every side except for an opening in the front that we'd be able to view the television through. The remainder of the blankets and pillows got shoved into the fort. With an outstretched arm I gestured for her to enter.

"Ladies first."

She curtsied, then crawled inside, and I clumsily followed with popcorn in tow after putting in the DVD and grabbing every remote. There wasn't a great deal of room, but we managed to sit a few inches apart in opposite corners with our backs to the foot of the couch.

"Get pumped up for this masterpiece you are about to witness. The makeup is excessive and the musical numbers are unnecessary."

She glanced over at me. "Stop making excuses for the thing if you love it so much."

And with that I shrugged and pressed Play.

TEN

ASHLINN WAS completely absorbed from the second the 20th Century Fox logo popped up in glorious Technicolor. I didn't have the heart to fast-forward through the opening credits. Not staring at her was difficult. There's only so long you can look at someone out of the corner of your eye without going dizzy, so I allowed my head to tilt toward hers as I watched her wonderment. It was humbling to know that someone who could bring about so many miracles was thrilled by one of our silly entertainments.

When "You Were Meant for Me" began playing, I could see she was being sucked in by the overly cheesy romanticism of it all. The tone changed for that single scene, and blue light emanating from the screen bathed our little sanctuary in an aqueous glow. Usually I would be bored by that particular dance, but watching her watch it was invigorating.

She had been gradually inching closer to my side, so I eased her journey and sidled up to her. Ashlinn's head took no time to find its way to my shoulder after that, and by the next scene, my arms were around her. During the following number, she used me as a backrest instead of the couch, and my legs were curled around her waist like a belt. No one had ever allowed me to get so close before, and it was already an addiction.

Each long song seemed to stretch into the next millennium, and time ran like dripping honey. I wrapped myself tighter around her, and she squeezed my arm, still completely absorbed in the action onscreen. There were flappers and mobsters and colors so bright it was obviously right after the time of black-and-white cinema. The film concluded with a kiss, and when the credits began rolling, Ashlinn unwrapped my legs and arms from where they were around her and spun in my lap so her heady grin was now pointed in my direction.

"That was brilliant," she told me, and I wondered if she could get any more perfect.

"So are you," I responded, and she rewarded me with another tiny kiss on the nose.

"Where'd the popcorn go?"

I looked around and saw it spread on the floor like a lumpy constellation.

"It appears we spilled it, must've been during the maneuvering. That won't be fun to clean up later."

I kicked the toppled bowl farther away—there was only so much more damage to be done at that point—and brushed away the popcorn. The mess could be dealt with later, maybe the next morning. As long as I got it before Mother came home, I'd be good.

I had no idea what the time of day was and couldn't see out the curtained windows from the fort. Dragging her down with me, I lay back so her head was on my chest. Our feet stuck out of the front.

The credits rolled on in the background, and we both stared at the blanket ceiling above. I loved holding her in my arms, but everything seemed to be working out too well. There had to be a catch-22. Things never just sorted themselves out in my life. She sighed contentedly and drew lazy circles over my hand with her fingers.

"Is this truly enough for you?" I whispered, not wanting to ruin the mood enveloping the moment.

"Of course it is. More than enough."

"You don't want sex? You don't mind not kissing me?"

She turned her head and gave me a kiss on the clavicle. "I just did."

"You know what I mean."

Ashlinn was silent, then rolled off me and turned onto her stomach. With arms crossed beneath, her gaze raked over my appearance.

"I'd be happy to just watch movie musicals with you for the rest of eternity. Sex doesn't faze me. Too much of my time has been spent building obscene situations for it to freak me out at all. Being a voyeur to the minds of unconscious civilians has proven a great many things, and one of them is my sexuality."

She stopped talking and pondered for a bit. Her words were slow and seemingly hard to come by. "I guess I'm just more interested in other stuff."

"Other stuff?"

"Well, this is nice, the cuddling. And I like holding your hand and leaning against you. It appears contact is something we both like. I refuse to be pressured into sex, and I don't want to disappoint you, but it seems like that's not really something you want either."

"No, I don't think it is."

The idea of sex was vaguely repugnant and not having to squash those thoughts immediately was pleasant and brought a smirk to my face. She liked being in my arms, and I liked wrapping them around her. This would work.

I began to run my fingers through her short, coarse hair. She all but melted into my touch. Bringing her head back down to my chest, I continued the soothing action and was grateful her hair wasn't long enough to get messed up under my ministrations.

"How do you feel?" I asked.

"Adored. Also a bit like a cat."

If she were one, she'd be a panther.

"How do you feel?" she asked in return.

"Understood."

We lay there, just breathing the same air and savoring that we had found each other, even though the universe laid so much in our way. Our shared need for intimacy without sex brought back an idea I had seen in the documentary all those days ago, but I was wary about broaching the subject. Caring for her and having her return the favor sounded like a lovely thing to build a relationship on, but fear did have a habit of getting out of control in my head once it began, so I kept quiet.

My hands had stopped their exploration of her head without my realizing it, and she gave a soft grunt of frustration.

"That was nice. I think I was almost asleep," she began, but stopped at seeing my face. "Hey, what's up?"

"I want to make you happy. I have some ideas, but they could all be stupid, and I have no way of figuring that out. There are things I want, even though there's not much of a reason to, and things I should want that I don't. I'm just trying to work it all out."

"I have had the privilege of sorting through an abundance of stupid ideas, some of which have belonged to you. Try me. Nothing could possibly be as idiotic as what got me out here to begin with." Her face was pressed into my chest, which muffled her already drowsy words.

My answer didn't seem to want to come out. I turned my head to the side and began examining the foot of the couch we were lying diagonal to.

"I was thinking tomorrow I could...," I began, but the sentence halted of its own accord.

She urged me on with a muttered "Yes?" and a tap on the stomach.

"I was thinking I could bathe you tomorrow morning. You know, like couples do, but without the sexy bits. Just being close to one another."

I hardly breathed the end of the sentence, ashamed of the admission for some reason. The self-consciousness vanished when my eyes were met with a pair full of amazement. It was as if I'd offered to fly her to the moon and back in a Ferrari-brand ship.

"That sounds perfect. Do please have ideas more often and share them frequently," Ashlinn urged.

"I'll certainly do my best."

"Great," she said, smiling sleepily at me. "Now I'm sorry to be such a killjoy, but I think I'm going to fall asleep soon."

"Already?"

"I've never actually had the pleasure of a night's rest before, so my apologies. Besides, it'll urge the morning on faster."

"Don't you want to go to bed?"

Lying on the floor wasn't awful, but it was a bit silly.

"I'm perfectly comfortable here. You can go retire to yours, though, if you're so inclined."

That was a laughable prospect. I just wrapped my arms around her tighter. She was out in seconds, completely unconscious, and her gentle snores filled the air like bubbles in champagne. I wondered if she was dreaming, experiencing the images she supplied to others. Maybe her mind was visiting with Reeves at that very moment, keeping him company and telling him the stories I used to be in charge of.

The credits had finished rolling a while ago, but I only noticed once Ashlinn was asleep. The screen was still lit and acted like a black night-light. Any other day I would have been terrified of monsters and memories lurking in the dark, but for this one moment everything was okay. Asexuality, auditions, and Ashlinn. The world was giving me reason to worship the A section of my dictionary.

The night swirled around me and every moment continued to drag on as my head began to feel foggier. My girlfriend's lethargic twitches broke up my thoughts as I willed sleep to take me. Her breath ghosted against my skin like a phantasmal caress until the static in my head lulled me to sleep. She did not meet me in any dreams, though, but instead left me to the will of Semira and her night terrors.

There was a man, a man on a motorcycle speeding down the road when a pack of cigarettes fell out of his pocket and onto the asphalt. I knew what was coming next and couldn't help but to watch, even though the need to stop everything was pulsating through my brain.

Upon realizing his accidental littering, he swung around dramatically to grab the box. I ran, but my legs didn't carry me toward the scene, and instead I just stayed in place like an old cartoon character, my limbs struggling frantically beneath me.

That's when the car came.

My father was driving with Reeves in the back, and I had no means of stopping him from trying to swerve around the biker reaching down in the middle of the road. No way of pushing the drugstore a bit to the right, leaving grass in its wake instead of a wall.

It was done.

Red metal folding up like an accordion against scarlet bricks, and that sound—like bass drums rolling into a gunmetal-gray dawn.

Before learning of Semira, I had always assumed nightmares to be a form of self-punishment, that my brain was attacking itself for one reason or another and the cause of the torment was internal. Knowing there was an actual being causing these destitute delusions did not make the situation any less unpleasant. My brain overflowed with a tailor-made horror, but I was freed from it by a hand on my shoulder and a shout in my ear.

Ashlinn had me held down by one arm and was bellowing.

"Wake up. I'm sorry. I'm so sorry." Her eyelashes stuck out in points making it look like she was wearing mascara.

"You're crying," I breathed, stroking her cheek with my thumb.

She wiped at her face and grasped my hand.

"So are you."

I had failed to notice my own tears and reaching up revealed that my face was soaked as well.

"It was just a nightmare."

She gave a little choked-off sob at my admission. I figured she already knew, judging by her need to awaken me, but hearing the words out loud must have brought a whole new level of truth to the situation. She couldn't stop the nightmares anymore. We both knew it was something I would have to deal with now, and Semira seemed desperate to make up for lost time. I just wished she would plague me with a different scenario. Ashlinn started apologizing again, but I shushed the girl and held her close. It was as much my fault as hers. In fact, it was completely my fault.

"Do you wish to talk about the nightmare?" she asked.

She was trying to find the right thing to say. I didn't want to rehash the screwed-up things that played endlessly behind my eyelids, but isn't that what couples do? Have pillow talk about their dreams? I gave it a try.

"It was the crash. The one that changed everything." Now I became conscious of my own tears and began to take heaving gasps between the words. "It's always the same thing, and it's ridiculous because I wasn't even there when it happened. I have no idea what it looked like, so how come I have the entire thing burned into my head like some goddamn catchy pop song?"

"Dreams that happen repeatedly do so for a reason. Maybe Semira is trying to help you figure something out."

"I'd appreciate it if she'd change her methods."

"I'm sorry I can't stop them from happening anymore." The regret was back in Ashlinn's voice.

"It's worth it to wake up next to you. Besides, now I know everything isn't all that bad with Reeves. That's comforting."

She smiled weakly at me, perhaps to show appreciation for my attempts to absolve her of blame. We looked like disasters, and neither of us was going to sleep again. Morning was approaching anyway, so I decided to continue the conversation instead of just lying there, stewing over the past.

"How was your first night sleeping? Any dreams of your own you wanna distract me with?"

"It was a singular experience. It wasn't really enjoyable, more like time travel to this moment. I had no dreams, which is a good thing because I'm not sure where they would have come from."

"Can't you make dreams for yourself?"

"Never tried. There isn't really the opportunity. I think the point of resting is that I don't have to engage in my day job."

I hummed in agreement.

The light coming in through the quilt's crocheted crevices was turning brighter by the minute, and I nudged her to say it was time to face the day. I did my best to unfold her from me, and we both clambered out of the makeshift tent, knocking over two blankets in the process and mangling the third. The nest beneath us had become a battlefield in the night and my legs were completely twisted in the sheets when I crawled away.

It took several minutes to extract every limb from our little haven. It wasn't a pretty sight to stand back and look at afterward, with popcorn strewn about like stiff confetti and the remains of what could have been a bedding store explosion. This would be something to deal with later. There were more pressing plans to occupy the morning with.

With a small dose of fear, I began pulling Ashlinn toward the bathroom.

"I have a promise to keep."

ELEVEN

SHE RUBBED her fingers over my palm as we walked through the dim house. The only lighting available came through slits in the blinds. It looked like the walls were bathed in gold leaf, and I hated to ruin it but was forced to turn on some lights to climb the staircase. Ashlinn thrummed with excitement behind me, and I was surprised I wasn't too anxious yet.

This is what adulthood must feel like. This is leaving the past behind and accepting the love of another. This is a balance. Or at least that's what I convinced myself of before it was time to actually do anything. We made it to the bathroom.

The room's yellow light was harsh, and I blinked against it before quickly turning to lay out the bath mat and turn on the shower, allowing the water to heat. An inkling of fear was creeping back again.

Does she like hot showers? How hot?

The realization that we'd have to be naked in order to take said shower caused the next wave of fear. For some reason I hadn't fully processed that before. Ashlinn had already been naked in my presence, so she shouldn't be too modest.

God, was that really just yesterday?

A lifetime had been compressed into the last hours, folded away into the meandering minutes. The last time we were in this bathroom together hadn't been for the best reasons. A trash can of drugs still sat in the corner. Upon noticing it I felt like I was experiencing hyperventilation of the mind.

Ashlinn pulled me from my anxious reverie by placing both hands on my shoulders.

"I might be wrong, but I doubt you want me to get your nice sundress soaked."

"Oh yeah, you're right," I stuttered. "You can take that off. I'll take mine off too, of course."

There was no reason to be so shy about this. People see their girlfriends naked all the time, and it's not like I had a body to be bashful about, being a dancer and all. The only thing I had any concerns with were my feet, with my inverted toes and odd veins. I didn't wear flip-flops for a reason.

She began taking off the sundress, leading the way as she had a tendency to do. It seemed only fair for me to follow suit, so I crossed my arms, took a deep breath, and reached down to the hem of my dress to pull it over my head. I didn't dare look at her. In my mind the tension was palpable, although it was likely she wasn't even affected.

When I finally stepped out of my underwear and looked up, her gaze was directed in the general vicinity of my head.

"Is it okay if I look at you?" she asked, as if there was any way to avoid the matter. Still, I appreciated the attempt at protecting my modesty. No turning back now.

"Go for it."

She nodded and gave me a once-over, a favor that I meekly returned. Her body sparked several reactions in me: admiration, appreciation, a vague feeling of smugness. Lust still didn't factor into anything, but this time I didn't try to force it.

The shower had turned warm and beckoning. Bravery was once again hers, and she grabbed my hand and pulled the curtain aside with her other hand before dragging me in. Ashlinn gasped when the water first hit her skin and released me, heading to the dryer end of the small shower.

"Oh no," I said before switching our positions and holding her directly under the spray of water. It ran in rivulets down her cheeks, and her mouth was an O of shock.

"It's so wet," she gasped, as if the idea personally offended her.

"I don't know what you expected."

She moved her head out of the water, revealing that her hair was suitably drenched.

I beckoned her a few inches forward, so that the water still pattered against her skin to keep the cold away, but her head was out of it.

"Close your eyes."

She wasn't looking when I almost dropped the shampoo bottle twice. I squeezed out far too much, used to washing my own longer locks.

"This shampoo probably isn't the best for curls," I apologized, running it over her scalp, "but it's all I've got."

I massaged the excessive amounts through her hair, piling the suds on her head as the shower filled with steam and the scent of cherry blossoms. Whenever the shampoo slipped toward her eyes, I rubbed the bubbles away with my thumb, and occasionally she'd give a contented sigh at my movements. I could focus on her hair only so long, though, and I was definitely prolonging the situation.

With a slight warning, I maneuvered her head under the water yet again and began rinsing. This was certainly on its way to becoming the longest shower ever taken, so I gave a silent prayer as the shampoo swirled down the drain that the hot water would last.

"You can open your eyes now."

She blinked and reached up to touch her hair.

"Does it feel any different?" I asked, amused.

"Not really. Just a bit soggy. Do you want me to return the favor?"

I had proposed the adventure to start with, so it was only fair that I let her do the same to me as I did to her, but the idea wasn't fitting in right in my head. Not unpleasant, but out of my still-growing comfort zone.

"Why don't you let me finish you up first?" I asked, and she nodded understandingly at my hesitance.

With bodywash in one hand, I grabbed her arm, which went limp in my grasp, and drew spirals on her with the soap. I repeated this with the other arm, then twirled my finger in front of her to indicate she should turn before I began working on her back and shoulders. With my front to her back I couldn't help wrapping my arms over her shoulders and just holding on.

For a few moments, it was just us in a perfect little tiled universe and endless summer rain. This nearness was something to build a life from. Eventually I pried myself away and spun her back around. Her expression was unbelievably calm, almost verging on comatose. Without really thinking, I fell to my knees before her and she lifted an eyebrow at me. I blushed, staring at the bottom of the tub.

"Don't get any ideas. I just wanted to do your legs."

Not daring to look up more than a foot above her ankles, I kept my head down and lathered her calves. When it was time to stand, my feet slipped, sending me sprawling backward. An expletive or two may have been shouted as I grappled with the edges of the tub to get up.

Well, that wasn't graceful. I really must have been a sight, awkwardly positioned in the corner of the tub with legs going in every direction. So much for intimacy.

"Are you okay?" Ashlinn asked with an edge of worry.

"Yeah. Just feel like an idiot."

She reached down to pull me up, and I graciously accepted her help as she dragged me to an upright position.

"That's the grace of a dancer," I joked, embarrassed. She squeezed my hands, and the water poured down on our connection.

"Hey there, dearie. Look at me."

My heart stuttered at the pet name, as did my lungs. So much care was pouring out of her expression.

"This has been absolutely wonderful," she assured me. "Thank you so much. No one has ever done anything like that for me before. I was doubtful they ever would."

"You don't have to doubt anymore."

She released my hands and quirked a smile. "No, I don't think I will."

And thus our adventure in the shower ended, with gratitude and a bruised elbow. I kicked the knob to turn the water off and reached out to grab a towel. After stepping onto the bath mat and unnecessarily helping her over the edge of the tub, I carefully patted her arms and ruffled the towel over her hair, something she pretended to be annoyed by. I might have believed her if it weren't for the giggling. I handed her the towel so she could finish the task and began drying off my own slightly less damp body.

She tied it around herself as a dress, then grabbed my towel. With one hand she threw it around my back to catch on the other side and used it to draw me forward before kissing each of my cheeks. Flashbulbs went off in my heart.

"You're too wonderful," I assured her, not knowing how I came to earn such affection.

"Well, I am a wet dream," she responded with a wink, and I groaned at the bad joke. She had obviously been waiting to say that.

"Not that I don't absolutely love standing here naked and soggy with you, but if we don't put clothes on soon, you'll end up getting sick, and I doubt I'd make the best nurse."

"You sell yourself short I'm sure, but I can see the point. Lead on."

After raiding my closet and making an even bigger mess of the house, she ended up in a sky blue sundress that went a bit long, and I donned a similarly cut floral print one. While she began trying to match together the shoes that were strewn about the bottom of my closet, she asked, "What's on the agenda for today?"

"Normally I'd say dance practice, but I think I can take a break now."

"Sounds fair enough."

She pulled out a pair of cloth flats that were scrunchy in the middle and tried them on. They fit well.

"Why don't we visit your father's resting place? I don't want my being here to interfere with your usual visits."

I couldn't tell whether or not she was testing me. This was a study in trust, on how much I'd let her in. My first impulse was to lock her out of this section of my life, but there was no way I could go on in such a manner. She was already acquainted with Reeves. It was only fair she should know of the man responsible for us both. There were parts of me I didn't want to share with her, but that didn't mean I wasn't going to.

My personality was hewn from unpleasant experiences, the car crash being one of them, and understanding them would be one way to understand me.

"Okay, let's go. First we have to cut some flowers for him from the garden. I'll get the shears; you can go pick what kind."

Maybe planning this trip to the graveyard was me testing her as much as the reverse. It was one way of seeing how true her feelings were.

She walked out the back door, trying to be discreet about her pleasure at my agreement as I headed to the garage. Shears were lying on top of the gardening gloves and seeds. They were used the most out of everything and rarely got buried beneath other gardening supplies. I grabbed them and jogged back through the house and out into the garden, disregarding everything I'd ever heard against running with sharp objects.

Ashlinn was standing among the gardenias and impatiens, looking very much like a mythical creature. Actually, she might just be a mythical creature.

She saw me on the pathetic trio of steps Mother wrongly called the porch and waved me over, then walked to another area of the garden. White carnations were blossoming at her feet.

"Let's bring these."

The carnations growing behind my house seemed plain in comparison to the one Reeves had gifted to me through her. I wondered if she had picked them because of that connection as I bent over and snipped the stems of a few flowers, making sure not to kneel to avoid getting dirt all over my knees. When I had four carnations to show for the effort, she took them and we walked through the house to the front sidewalk, grabbing my bag on the way. If some money just happened to vanish from Mother's emergency fund, that could be dealt with later. I had become determined to enjoy every second with Ashlinn as much as I could and spoil her if at all possible.

It was late enough in the morning that a fair number of people were dotting the sidewalks, although in comparison to New York they were hardly noticeable. If my town was a city, it was acoustic where Manhattan was electric with speakers. The dog walkers and joggers shot a few peculiar looks in our direction as they sluggishly completed their tasks, perhaps because of the mere fact I wasn't alone, but more likely because of Ashlinn's stunning and perhaps vaguely familiar appearance. You could almost see the déjà vu, but they all appeared to be too sleepy to acknowledge it. With how slowly everyone was moving, it was almost as if we had turned into a quaint little Southern town overnight.

Blaming the early morning for their slowness, we continued around two corners and across one street to the graveyard's underwhelming gate. I walked ahead of her, navigating us through the familiar turf, until we were standing only a bit away from my father's name. The sun shone warmly on my back and cast our shadows across his stone.

Without speaking she placed all of the carnations in a little stack at the foot of the grave, then stood behind me and wrapped an arm around my shoulder. The wind blew my hair to the side and away from her as it failed at cooling the nearly intolerable summer heat.

"What happened, exactly?" she asked, her voice barely louder than a whisper. "Reeves can't remember any details of the accident. He didn't even know your father had died. I've always been a bit curious."

I didn't answer for a few seconds, so she tacked a "You don't have to tell me now if you don't want to" on the end.

Bringing her here was difficult enough. No one ever came to the graveyard with me. It felt peculiar, like the memory of this visit would poke out roughly among the others. I almost felt as if I should be introducing my father to her. He probably would have liked Ashlinn, with her eccentricities and quirks, and now she wanted a play-by-play of the worst possible day. How do I go about describing my painful memories, especially when I wasn't even eyewitness to the actual event? No words could do such a thing justice, and it's unfair to tell the story and risk having it be misinterpreted. Still, I attempted to spin thoughts into syllables that meant more than any I had ever told a therapist.

"It really was a nasty crash. They went right into the side of a drugstore. We don't drive much here, as you've probably seen.

The town's just so small, but Reeves played baseball and the fields are too far away." My throat clenched, and I could feel the sting of fresh tears building up in my eyes, burning like the breeze. "He always wanted to sit in the front seat. He said everyone else his age was allowed, and he was probably right, but Dad still made him sit in the back. That's why he ended up living. Well, if you can call it that."

My voice had gone crackly at the end and I couldn't continue. Couldn't describe how the EMTs had pried him from the mangled car, which was little more than a clump of red painted metal by the time they arrived. How they must have realized my father was a lost cause. No one ever intended me to see the state of the car, the prison that held my family in their last moments, but it was hard to avoid when the next day it was on the front page of the local newspaper. My tears fell freely, streaking my cheeks, but there were no sobs. I was composed, used to this pain.

Ashlinn wrapped her other arm around me and placed her chin on my shoulder. We stood there, breathing shakily for what felt like an age, until she eventually unwrapped herself and looked me in the eyes. I nodded with finality and blurry vision. We walked away from my father and out the gate, our shadows shrinking against the stone until it was left completely in the light.

TWELVE

"LET'S GET some food," I said, and she perked up at the mention of it. "There's a diner down the road that shouldn't be packed with too many old people."

There were several reasons to bring her out to eat, some of which were my intense lack of cooking abilities, something she was not yet privy to; pancakes; and her reaction to said pancakes. Now I just had to hope there was enough money in my bag.

The diner was a small building with metallic walls and one red stripe wrapping around the top. When we entered, a little bell above the door jangled and some patrons lazily turned their heads toward us from where they sat in worn chairs at disgustingly patterned tables. There was a single television that must have been on some sort of rest mode because it was just showing a looping video of fish in a plasticized tank.

A woman with dyed red hair piled high on her head walked out of the kitchen's swinging doors. She was heavyset, yet could navigate between the tight booths flawlessly.

"Victoria!" she exclaimed. "Haven't seen you here for ages."

I couldn't recall ever having known this woman, but that's life when your town's a single square mile of nosy neighbors and the elderly.

"Yeah, I've been busy." Sometimes even true excuses are lame.

The lady smirked at me. She wasn't buying that there was anything more worth taking up my time than visiting some diner on a regular basis.

"I'll just show you and your friend to a table."

We ended up crammed in one of the few booths for two all the way in the corner. About 90 percent of the table was covered in either condiments or jelly, and I could barely see Ashlinn over the "Specials" card protruding from the middle of this display. She was flipping through the menu with a thoughtful look on her face, nodding every couple of seconds as her eyes roamed over the words. It was absolutely adorable.

"You have no idea what you want, do you?" I asked her, grinning. She dropped the menu immediately.

"Thank God you noticed. You can pick for me. I trust you have it figured out better than I do."

The waitress returned after seeing us lower our menus, and I ordered two chocolate milks and blueberry pancakes. She didn't question my ordering for the both of us, but the woman's gaze did seem to linger on Ashlinn for an uncomfortable length of time as she inched away, scooting around the corner to the kitchen.

Reeves's favorite thing had been chocolate milk. He got two cartons of it every lunch in school and made it almost on a daily basis at home. He'd pour in chocolate until the cup was near overflowing and stirred it into a concoction so dark it might as well have been straight syrup. It seemed a fitting drink for Ashlinn to try.

The counter was packed with harried men hunched over cups of coffee. Many cups of coffee. There were about the same number empty as there were full, all arranged in front of them as a sort of caffeinated connect-the-dots.

"Turn the television on," one of them demanded gruffly. "Wanna see how last night's game turned out."

Our chocolate milks arrived. Ashlinn didn't even bother to use her straw and instead just downed a third of the glass in a few impressive gulps. I watched her throat muscles working and felt a surge of happiness that I was actually in a relationship with someone. It was like an epiphany. The most perfect girl I could fathom was sitting across from me in a world outside of my head, and she would never pressure me into anything. Maybe we weren't broken after all.

I tapped my straw against the table to ease the paper off, then slipped it into my glass. As I swirled it around, scraping off the chocolate sauce from the inner edges, the man at the counter was attempting to work a television remote. Obviously he was having issues figuring out how to turn off the endlessly swimming fish and put on an actual program. A part of me wished some waitress would come by and have pity on him.

Ashlinn finally put the drink back down and stared at me.

"I got really lucky," she said conversationally. "Not only can my girlfriend dance and look unbelievably cute all the time, but she has really fantastic taste in beverages and amazing popcorn abilities, not to mention she thinks I'm great."

"She really does."

I wanted to cry (again). I wanted to tell her it wasn't true, that I was actually the lucky one in the situation. But then I realized, maybe both of us really were the lucky ones. Her judgment was not to be disagreed with.

"Hey, tell me about our waitress," I said, leaning over the table conspiratorially, recalling how Ashlinn rattled off facts about the wannabe actor in New York.

"What about her?"

"I dunno. Maybe that she's an ex-assassin who wants to open a space-themed go-go bar."

We both looked over at the woman and laughed as she almost knocked over a glass of orange juice with her frankly impressive posterior.

"Actually, she's quite happy as she is. Growing up, that woman wanted to be around people who'd recognize her on a daily basis, give her a nickname, and call her sweetheart. I'd say that's worked out. If I remember correctly, her happiest day occurred with a young gentleman at a camp in Ohio. Sometimes when I'm feeling lazy, I'll give her recurring dreams about him."

"Wow. Can you really do that with anyone?"

There was no schooling the amazement from my voice. It was like a magic trick with nothing up the sleeves. She blushed a bit at my praise and scanned the diner.

"Most everyone, yeah. It's what I do. Glad you find it amusing."

That moment was perfect. We were floating through time, tethered to reality by the clattering sounds of a small-town diner. Her kind words could carry me home; they could spin dreams and mend miracles, but they could not preserve our happy state of being for longer than a single flawless juncture in time. Because that's when the news flashed on.

A monotone newscaster voice came from the screen to our left, and the woman's fuzzy words made the tight space seem even more cramped. The television had come to life as the woman was in the middle of a sentence, and we all looked up at the sound.

"A cause has yet to be found for the recent plague of nightmares and the ensuing insomnia. Scientists have been testing the water supply in several parts of the country in a search for answers, but results have so far been inconclusive." There was a beat. Silence.

Oh God. This can't be a coincidence.

I began to look back toward Ashlinn, eyes wide with fear, but she was already out of her seat. In a few steps she was next to the man wielding the remote, and snatched it before he could figure out how to change the channel.

"Hey, darlin', give that back," he said but gave up quickly once she shushed him, her eyes glued to the screen. He didn't put up much of a fight, but that fact suited his haggard appearance. Actually, looking around, everyone did seem exhausted. Bloodshot eyes and shaking fingers. All that coffee.

I rushed over to where Ashlinn stood and grabbed her with one hand while throwing the other over my mouth. Do I convince her it has nothing to do with us? Demand she explain what the hell is going on?

Everyone was slouching, leaning their heads in their hands. She turned the volume up minutely, and there was a slight collective groan. How did we miss this? The screen showed images of exhausted students, people falling asleep on benches. Civilians were on the street describing their awful night terrors. There hadn't been a good dream in two days.

"Maybe there *is* something in the water," I tried to tell her, not believing the words.

"I knew this would happen. I knew, and I ignored it. We have to go now."

Her tone was frantic and left little room for denial. She was squeezing my hand tighter by the second, and it was almost starting to hurt. Her eyes were beginning to glaze over as if to premeditate tears.

"Okay. Can we eat first?"

Ashlinn looked up at me as a single tear began its journey down her cheek, so I retracted my previous question and dragged her to the front without even waiting for a response, only turning to grab my purse on our way. Food could wait. I threw a twenty onto the front counter, which housed the cash register, hoping they'd understand and maybe give some poor, exhausted bastard free pancakes later. The bell sounded more like an alarm as we rushed back out the front door, our chocolate milks left unfinished on the table behind us.

Ashlinn was quick to release my hand and start jogging, but I didn't let her get too far ahead on the sidewalk as we made our way home.

"Call Ellie," she said between breaths as we turned the corner, "I need to talk to someone other than you about this."

"Let's wait 'til we get home at least. Maybe the people on the news are an anomaly of some sort. Blame aliens or dieting."

"Did you see everyone in the diner? And those people walking their dogs this morning? This is a bigger issue than you can even begin to understand, my dear."

I was beginning to take the lead in our little impromptu running race, considering I actually knew the way home. When we arrived she barely slowed upon walking through the door. Ashlinn reached into my bag and dug violently for the phone. She began pressing buttons wildly, and my only demand was that she put it on speaker. This conversation was too important to be locked out of. At least she didn't keep a door between us this time.

We stood in the middle of the floor as the phone rang out in Ashlinn's hand. She was tapping her foot erratically and wouldn't meet my eyes. The other line picked up, and Ellie's voice came fuzzily.

"What's up now?"

"How have you been sleeping recently?"

"Oh hi, Ashlinn. Wow, you just cut to the chase, don't you? How is this any of your business? Shouldn't you guys have more interesting things to be getting up to, if you know what I mean?"

She deepened her voice at the end of the sentence, and before I could mention Ellie's blatant innuendo, Ashlinn just told her to "Answer the question. Please." She sounded worn out. Brittle.

"Okay, okay. To tell you the truth, I've been running on energy drinks for the past day. I mean, I've had enough Monsters to make someone's heart implode. The night before New York, I kept having these crazy nightmares, and it must've scared me more than I realized 'cause I didn't sleep at all last night. Not that you guys had that issue, I'm sure."

Ellie sounded like she was about to say more, but Ashlinn had already hung up and dropped the phone on my bedside table.

With nothing in her hands, it was like she didn't know what to do with them. They were clenching, and she kept moving as if to rend her hair, then let them drop to her sides. My girlfriend was a fidgeting mess, falling to pieces in my living room as I did little apart from standing there with a stricken expression. Someone had to speak, so I let slip the truest thought bobbing through my head at the time.

"I don't understand."

She looked up at me with pained eyes.

"I have to leave now. You get that, right?" Her voice was breaking almost as much as my heart.

"No."

"I have to. All these people who aren't sleeping, who are having nightmares, that's my fault." She clutched at her short curls of hair, and I feared she would hurt herself.

"No," I repeated.

"Do you want everyone to become an insomniac? I shouldn't have come here so impulsively. And you," she said, pointing at me wildly, "you've been so distracting. There's been no one to balance out Semira without me, and I never even realized."

"No!" This time I screamed that single syllable as I reached out to remove her fingers from where they gripped her head. "Find another way. Can't you do both? Make dreams and stay with me? I don't even understand what's going on. Just tell Semira to back off."

"I wish it was that easy. I'm like a light switch: dream or human. Being both is too much effort, and Semira is not to be trifled with. She's a bit like Ellie, with a mind of her own and the willpower to match."

"I'm not going to lose you. Please. I've already lost so much it isn't fair. You're the happiest thing that's happened to me in a long time, and I can't give this up."

Sadness rolled off her, and my words only succeeded in making the scene even more despondent.

"Oh, sweetie, so many happy things happen to you. Maybe you just haven't been paying enough attention." She reached out for me, a gesture I felt undeserving of, and our arms formed a bridge between us.

"I'm not sure if I want any of those happy things if they aren't you, and I'm still confused about my wanting you."

"There isn't another option. People could die if I don't become a dream again. I've been playing hooky long enough."

"Fine," I blurted when a realization struck, "get back to work, but take me with you. Make me a dream too."

She was already shaking her head, but I continued regardless.

"I'll help you do whatever it is you do, and we can walk through memories together. We can visit my brother every day. I won't be leaving much behind. I'd rather be with you."

"You have so much to look forward to. I can't take that away no matter how tempting it sounds. College, love. Your mother needs you. This glittering reality is so wonderful. It suits you. Besides, I doubt Reeves would be thrilled to hear of you giving up everything he could have had."

What could I say? That was a point we both knew I could never argue with. He had had his childhood stolen, and I was ready to give up the rest of mine.

When we were younger, Reeves and I would always hold our breath during scenes in movies where characters couldn't breathe. One time *Titanic* was on television. We only started watching near the end when things got interesting. Well, Jack was diving underwater to pick something up, and we both puffed out our cheeks and covered our mouths. The need for oxygen was stronger than any lust in my life, but glancing over at Reeves showed that he still wasn't breathing, and I refused to let the boy win. He was probably just taking shallow breaths through his nose without my noticing. With stubbornness I refused to let any air in my lungs until my head went fuzzy, like cotton swabs were rubbing away at the edges of my mind. That was the last time I feared passing out, and the uncomfortable feeling was back.

Carefully, I brought us to the couch and sat down.

"We were so happy yesterday." Those words were the sound of me giving up.

Ashlinn smiled at me, but it didn't reach her eyes.

"I'm not sure if I've ever been happier."

"If you stay, we can have an entire life of yesterdays." I could feel the desperation in my voice but knew no way of stopping it. "We can see so many places. I swear the world is twice as beautiful through your eyes."

"It won't be beautiful any longer if I let this go on. How could I possibly be happy when Semira is out there ruining everyone else's lives? I've seen the memories of all these people, their hopes and goals. I care about them. Not to mention she's been hurting you as well. Those nightmares last night will not be a one-time occurrence if this continues."

"I can handle the nightmares."

What the hell is going on with this Semira woman? If it weren't for her, surely we could stay as we are. Why does everything have to be ruined? Happiness should come with a warranty. Maybe this lady can be reasoned with.

"How about this: take me to meet Semira. We'll go into a dream together; you can do that, right? I'll try to reason with her. We can talk. You said she wasn't all bad."

Ashlinn looked doubtful, but I could see some hope seeping through.

"That's true, but she's also confused and very misguided."

"Aren't we all? Look, you want me to start making good decisions for myself. That's part of the reason you came to start with. Let me do this, please. I've already lost too many people I love."

She was definitely thinking it over, and I already knew I'd won. Our pull over each other went both ways.

"Fine. Here's the plan: when you go to sleep, I'll enter your dream and beckon Semira to us and maybe allow you two to speak. I'll find out why she's running rampant with the nightmares and see if we can knock some sense into the woman." Her tone was pessimistic, and in the time we'd known each other she had never looked so unsure, but I felt beyond victorious.

"Thank you so much," I squealed, practically rolling on top of her in a botched attempt at a hug. "Now we have the whole day before us too."

"We shouldn't let it linger. It will probably be our last together," she reminded me, and I deflated.

"Don't speak like that," I begged, squeezing her.

I draped myself over her shoulders as her arms snaked around my waist. It felt safe in her embrace, and she still smelled like summer nights. This was acceptance, not of her but of myself. Our foreheads were so close we were breathing the same air. Who needs kissing when you can share oxygen?

"You're the most fantastic thing that has ever happened to me, and I won't even be able to talk about you to anyone."

"Nor will I. There's always Reeves, but I doubt he'd want to be privy to such intimate information about his dear sister."

I felt vaguely horrified at her telling my brother anything about our romantic life, regardless of its lack of physicality.

"You wouldn't dare," I growled, and she laughed, although her heart was obviously not in it. That was a tragedy in itself.

I pulled her in tight as if it were my intention to absorb her—not that it would be a bad idea because then nothing would be able to steal her away—and rubbed circles into her shoulder blades. This could have continued indefinitely if my stomach hadn't rumbled.

"Sorry, we skipped lunch," I said as an excuse, and she gave me a half smile and started to pull me toward the kitchen. "Is it bad I could honestly care less about eating right now?" I asked her, although it wasn't really the truth. "I can eat any day, but who knows how much time I have left with you? I can manage."

She ignored my protests and began rummaging through the cabinets.

"If you learn one thing from my being here, I hope it's that there's little more important than caring for that body of yours. Sacrificing yourself for stupid reasons isn't okay, not that we're a stupid reason or anything. Case in point, you need to eat. Besides, you took care of me. It's about time I return the favor."

There would be no coercing the girl, so I decided to make the most of it.

"Ramen's to your left," I told her before taking a seat to watch.

THIRTEEN

SHE READ through the instructions on the back of the package several times before even opening it, and neatly placed the brick of noodles right in the center of a plate rescued from the cabinet. Then she laid the seasoning packet squarely next to it, and the still intact instructions remained in her grasp as she searched for a pot and measuring cups.

I had never actually heard of someone measuring the amount of water to boil for instant noodles, but she did just that, and the measurements were extremely precise judging by how she got eye level with the cup. I almost interrupted her cooking, but it seemed better to allow her to do this however she deemed best.

She slowly poured the water into a small pot and lit the stove beneath it. Her eyes never left the water as she waited for it to boil, and I held back any observations about watched pots. I tried to commit certain details of her physicality to memory, like her stature. This might be my last chance to do so, and even blinking seemed like a waste of time. The way she held herself was an art form. She was doing something with the noodles and a wooden spoon, but I was too busy trying to sear the image of her obsidian curls into my memory to really pay any attention. I hadn't even realized she finished until the still steaming water was being poured down the drain.

We sat at the round kitchen table with our chairs pulled up as close to one another as we could manage, two forks and a single bowl of ramen being shared between us. Our arms were pressed against each other and I kept laying my head on her shoulder between bites. This wasn't something I could fathom ever doing with anyone else. No friend had ever been this close. This really was a romantic relationship.

"You know," I said, barely louder than a whisper, "I don't think I mind being asexual."

"Then the time I spent being human means more than I dared hope."

The noodles were gone, but neither of us moved. We just sat there, lost, using each other for support.

Finally, Ashlinn screwed up her courage and spoke. "Might as well get this over with. Let's go talk to Semira."

We went to my room, figuring it would be easier for me to succumb to sleep if I was actually in a bed instead of on the floor. It was a good excuse not to revisit the site of our slumber party; that would surely not have been a pretty sight.

In the bathroom I changed into the pajamas I had been wearing when Ashlinn first appeared in my bed, although there was little reason not to undress in front of her.

She had placed a chair next to the bed in my absence. It might as well have been a guillotine blade.

"No way," I insisted, glaring at the chair like it was something lethal. "You're lying down with me."

I tried to instill every ounce of surety into that one statement. My arms were even crossed to further show my resolve.

"What's the point?" she asked with her hands clutching the top. "It's not as if I'm going to be sleeping."

"Even more reason for you to hold me, dammit. It might be our only chance. If I'm going to go the rest of my life untouched, I need to stock up now."

That seemed to be enough because she silently pushed the chair to the side with a nod and shut off the lights. Everything was still completely visible in the sunshine coming through the blinds, and she climbed into bed after me, which felt like a reversal of her first night in this world.

"I don't think I'll be able to fall asleep very quickly like this. It's still early," I told her, pulling the comforter up over us. There was no pretending I was upset by the extra time I believed we would inevitably have to spend together.

"Don't worry."

I wasn't, but I let her continue.

"I have a plan."

She spooned up behind me, and I felt the situation should have been a lot more uncomfortable than it truly was. There was a certain level of safety in her arms. With her head nuzzled up behind me, she brought magic into reality.

First she whispered, "I love you and won't let this be the end."

Oh God, I should have been the first to say it. I wanted nothing more than to return the sentiment. Someone loved me, and it wasn't out of obligation. They dug beneath the scars and low IQ. This is what I tried to express with my dancing.

Then before I could even open my mouth to respond like I so desperately wanted to, she began humming a single note. The tone was so low and deep it seemed to relax every muscle in my body. I hadn't realized how tense I was. My head was getting heavier and sinking deeper into the pillow by the second. It was so plush and welcoming, but I didn't want to sleep. I wanted to revel in those three words. The second that humming met my ears, though, I was teetering on the foggy area between asleep and waking. In no time I was out cold.

Bright bursts tore through the darkness of my mind.

Fireworks.

I was in a stadium of some sort, and fireworks were exploding into a supernova of glitter that rained down like blessings. Much in the way of blessings, they also failed to reach their destination. I heard a deafening bam followed by a worn-out fizzing sound, and it seemed to stick in my ears after the lights faded. Looking around the stadium revealed only empty seats and a vacant field. Dread chilled my skin.

"Ashlinn?"

My stammering voice was swallowed up by silence.

The sky kept lighting up in a sickening display of color, and I spun around on the large concrete stairs, not feeling safe with my back turned anywhere. At the top of the staircase stood a hot dog cart and an abandoned gift shop. They were only visible when the fireworks went off. I continued turning uncomfortably, scanning the seats, until I faced the field again.

I was not alone. And Ashlinn was not the one keeping me company.

An elderly woman was two steps down from me with the unnatural black hair that comes from boxed dye. A murky brown robe covered in different sized, clear buttons hung off her shoulders.

A gun was pointed at me with near translucent skeletal fingers clutched around the trigger. Those fingers belonged to her.

Something was off about the whole situation, apart from the geezer with a gun. The air was sick and every seat seemed distant, like I would never be able to reach them even if I ran. I tried, but my feet felt like cinder blocks and I remained immobile. In a similar manner, my vocal cords forgot their purpose, and all hope of screaming for help was lost. My entire world was the barrel of a gun.

There was another bam like before, except this one was not followed by a fizzing sound. Light did appear, but it was much more focused and erupted only from the point my eyes were locked on. As if in slow motion, I saw the bullet launch and twist in the air toward my heart. The fear culminated in my immobile body as metal tore through bone and the surrounding flesh.

Then there was nothing.

My body was floating in a gray oblivion. It was edgeless and claustrophobic all at once. My soul spiraled there for what could have been ages when Ashlinn's voice cut through the emptiness, tethering me to something.

"Stop it, you're going to make her wake up! Stop this right now, Semira."

Her voice was muffled, but she was definitely shouting.

Exiting that abyss was like being sucked down a drain that squeezed and stretched as you filtered through, and on the other side was a room as white as my brother's hospital. Unlike the hospital, though, there was no visible ceiling. Or any patients, for that matter. Just the culmination of every color of the rainbow into one uncomfortably bright, blank canvas.

Ashlinn was standing there, glaring at the old lady who had lost the gun after I failed at losing my life. I desperately wanted to run to my girlfriend and demand an explanation, but my feet still felt heavy, so I merely stared and attempted to puzzle out the situation at hand.

"You're okay, Victoria. I must assure you I never intended for that to happen," Ashlinn told me, her eyes never leaving that woman. It reminded me of nature shows where they warn the viewers to not drop their gaze when facing a predator. "We wanted to ask you a favor. I know you are a kind woman but recently things have been getting out of hand. We were hoping a compromise could be made."

Ashlinn walked over and took my stiff hand.

"Don't you have anything to say, Victoria?" She was looking at me hopefully, and I tried to organize my sensible thoughts among the still lingering memories of fear.

Why is this important? Right. Ashlinn is going to leave. Nightmares.

Some girl named Semira is giving everyone nightmares.

With a shock I realized the old woman had to be the tormentor in question, haggard appearance and all. I'm not sure what I expected, maybe another teenaged beauty. Instead, the foil to Ashlinn's powers was someone who looked minutes away from being tossed into a retirement home. She was standing before us, sentinel still with those fragile hands clasped behind her back. I'll give the woman one thing, for such a feeble-looking lady, her posture was impeccable.

"Well," I began, partially as a bid for more time, "this is Semira?"

"Of course she is."

"Of course I am." Her creaky voice came from every direction. There would be no pinning down its origin if it weren't for her moving lips. She redirected her attention from me to Ashlinn, allowing her gaze to linger over our linked hands.

"You haven't been doing your job. I was going to ask why, but I suppose the explanation is standing right in front of me. Funny, I never took you to be the caring type."

Ashlinn's hand clenched angrily around mine. "You barely even know me."

"No, I suppose I don't, but we are one and the same. Entities who exist solely to do the best for people like her. Or at least, you used to hold their best interests in mind. Tell me, is she worth all the suffering you are causing?"

Ashlinn didn't answer. She just stared straight ahead. This woman didn't just toy with her guilt. As if that weren't bad enough, there was more.

"Wait, I think I've figured this out. She's a freak like you, isn't she? Scared of sex and not willing to try. A shame, truly. A pretty girl such as yourself would have made many men so very happy. Just imagine the fantasies. Still, no wonder you got attached to this one. Feeling like less of a mistake is obviously more important than the exhausted parents dealing with screaming infants at the witching hour."

Semira was dancing around as she spewed these words, her movements looking downright improbable. I wanted to shout out that it wasn't the way she said at all and to please shut up, but instead I distilled my disgust into carefully picked words. That was the reason for this endeavor to begin with and our only chance.

"We love each other so much, and you don't need to understand the way we show it to know it's true. Look at us. The idea of never seeing her again makes me feel like I'm drowning. Please just tone it down with the nightmares. There's no reason for them to continue, and we're not asking you to stop completely. Just go back to normal. If the world can sleep, we can be together, and you'll never have to deal with our freakishness again." The ending I had tacked on with a fair amount of spite, but it seemed justified. Not that Semira noticed. Actually, I had barely gotten out the first sentence when she began laughing with closed lips and twinkling eyes.

After regaining the little she had lost of her composure, she said, "Oh, sweetie, there must always be a balance. Good and bad, yin and yang, night and day. All those clichés. I got the poor side of the deal, but that doesn't mean I can't enjoy it. Every hour I get to sift through such beautiful pain, while your love is on the opposite side of the spectrum. She should be more grateful."

Ashlinn was still looking at the indistinguishable floor, and I would have thought she was frozen if it weren't for the little twitch she gave when Semira sarcastically barked out the word love. She got to hear that word from her before me. The dreadful woman wouldn't stop talking.

"Even if I did lighten up, there would still be nothing but nightmares and no one to make the pleasant dreams. Ashlinn knows this; returning to our realm is inevitable. Think of all the mothers who can no longer wish their children 'sweet dreams' before bed."

As Semira glided toward us, Ashlinn wrapped her arms around me. She was muttering the word sorry over and over, and I wasn't certain who this apology was directed at. The old woman stopped and crossed her arms.

"You think I can't judge you, that I don't know you, but does she?" Semira jabbed her finger in my direction as she spoke to Ashlinn. "How can you think she loves you if she doesn't even know you?"

I was shaking my head until Ashlinn placed her hand in my hair and leaned me against her shoulder. Her lips touched the top of my head as Semira's voice hit us from every angle, still sounding as if it were resonating off absent walls.

"Your girlfriend will suffer. There is no reason for her not to succumb to my night terrors, and you know it. You've seen her as monsters unfurl behind closed eyes. You've seen her helpless. If you remain human those visions will be coming for both of you. Now I can see your fears too, Ashlinn. Don't forget that."

As she spoke the room transformed, and Ashlinn jumped away from me in surprise, jostled by the changing setting. Mirrors rose from the shaking floor, concealing Semira behind them. They arranged themselves in front of us in a sort of half-octagonal shape. It reminded me of changing rooms in high-end clothing stores.

We were reflected in all of them, but only Ashlinn's reflection was honest. In every mirror I stood next to her but was different each time. My actual actions had no control over the doings of this evil twin.

In the first one, I was angled away from her with a bottle of pills, downing them as if they were Skittles. In the next I merely stood there, staring straight ahead with hollow eyes jutting out from dark circles. My arms dangled limply, and the whole picture was zombie-like.

The images got progressively sicker from left to right as my false reflection began making contact with Ashlinn. I was shown shoving at her angrily and turning away repeatedly, leaving bruises and God knows what else.

The last mirror disgusted me so much I couldn't settle on whether to vomit or cry, and just ended up standing there, paralyzed. I wanted to hold Ashlinn, to promise it was all an illusion, but that seemed impossible after viewing such a sight.

There I was, biting at Ashlinn's neck and rubbing up against her, my hands finding their way down her stomach and toward her crotch. My reflection wasn't being kind about it. Ashlinn never claimed to be sex-repulsed, but this was masked molestation. The false Victoria must have heard a disapproval of some sort, because the next thing I knew a hand was coming across Ashlinn's face in a manner that could never be construed as gentle. It was impossible to look at and I almost wanted to saw off my own hands in punishment.

The whole time, Ashlinn's reflection remained true to how she was standing, and her face looked half-dead as she watched. Empty eyes and stoic chin. No escape.

"Stop it!" I screamed, just like Ashlinn had after my false shooting. "Stop this right now!"

Ashlinn gasped and looked to me with an absolutely shattered expression, her no-longer-dead eyes sparking with fear, and began holding up a hand as if to stop me, but it was too late. A creaky voice said, "Okay," and the dream began to crumble apart. It disintegrated into gray birds and flew away, leaving me awake. And completely alone.

FOURTEEN

MY HANDS fumbled through the sheets that still smelled of summer from when Ashlinn had lain in them however long ago, and I threw the comforter around viciously in the dark.

No. God, no.

And that's when I saw it: her sundress lying limp and crumpled in the space she had previously occupied.

It couldn't end like that. I refused to let everything be over. Surely Ashlinn would come back soon and explain everything. She'd visit me in a dream; maybe the whole thing was just a nightmare, and she was downstairs right now.

My body wasn't as hopeful as my mind, judging by the tears blurring this emptier world. Just another case of me unintentionally making things more difficult for myself. I grabbed a flashlight, regardless of the fact I could turn on the lights, and began running around the house praying she'd be hiding out somewhere. I never even got to say a proper good-bye, and now the last image to remember her by was a haunting one. I'd have flashbacks to that moment forever.

Those images, the despair on Ashlinn's face—it all kept flickering behind my eyes like something out of a children's flip-book. Every heartbeat was infected with the memory, spreading it through my body like a poison.

She told me she loved me.

I barely made it to the bathroom before I began vomiting. My body turned back on itself and every muscle was trying to snap as my midriff inverted. Talking to Semira had been a horrible decision. Ashlinn was gone, and we didn't even get to part on a positive note, our last moment tainted by the unspeakable. Maybe what I never got to say would manifest itself in my hopes. That way she'd see them when sorting through dream material.

Did she know I loved her too? She had to. My belief was the only proof, though.

If she could forgive me, I would consider forgiving myself. There was nothing left but to carry on, although that didn't mean I wanted to do it. Being sick in the bathroom got me started cleaning, allowing myself a chunk of time to recuperate. The garbage can of medicine was still standing in the darkened corner, mocking me. From the bathroom I stumbled downstairs and into the living room, still on a hopeless search.

There lay the pile of blankets from the other night, and I collapsed into them, whispering her name as I gave myself over to debilitating sobs. That night was so happy and so recent, but this last dream was acting as a barrier in my memory. How could I ever recall Ashlinn's astonishment at Gene Kelly when her horrified eyes were still on my mind? She couldn't be gone; this couldn't be it for my love life.

Every patter against the window or gust of wind turned into her tread to my ears, but she didn't come to take me into her arms. There were to be no more conversations or soul baring in person. No more Reeves. Even if she still came to me in dreams, touching her would never be the same. While crying every tear my body had to offer, I made up my mind to down some Nyquil—maybe if I could dream she'd visit me there—but when I calmed and my tears were a mere trickle, this idea became tasteless again. She said I deserved better than the drugs. I could respect that. After all, everything else Ashlinn told me had been worthwhile.

It was nearing morning and the world seemed to be thrumming painful tunes. The time I had spent asleep wasn't life-changingly long, and yet in that time, the dearest parts of me were snatched away. People should come prepackaged, with handy little labels.

Warning: This person will show you that you aren't a freak. They will make you feel loved. Then they will leave.

I was exhausted, but there was no chance of falling back asleep, not that I had a great desire to do anything other than lie down and wallow in despair. I was nothing but hormones and bad judgment.

"Come back," I whispered to the suffocating air. "Please."

Only the morning birds responded with distant chirping until motorcycles began revving at this ungodly hour, their roar silencing the song.

If only I could fall asleep. Make me into a computer to turn on and off until dreams of her form.

It was funny. I almost wanted to call Ellie. Tell her how it had finally happened: my first heartbreak. We could throw a party to mark my entrance into womanhood. Not that she counted what Ashlinn and I had as a proper relationship anyway. Avoiding that phone call was probably for the best, although she was much more well versed in matters of love than I could ever dream of being.

From my prison of sheets, I began wondering what day it even was. Monday? How long had she even been here? I thought back to the nights we had spent together and came to a numbing realization.

Mother!

I was running out of time to clean everything up. How the hell did I forget my mother would be coming back? Was today really the day? I counted off the nights in my bed. One, two, shit. Today was the day.

The collapsed blanket fort was weirdly comfortable, the closest thing I had to Ashlinn, but not putting the sheets and pillows back would lead to questions. My mentality was slowly improving, but even the most stoic person wouldn't be able to weather a cross-examination about this. Best to get rid of the evidence.

With the occasional break when my tears returned full force for a few minutes, I did away with the remnants of the fort and the scattered popcorn, as well as tidied the pots in the sink. The last two days might as well have been as imaginary as my dreams of her. Only the sundress knew the truth. That got folded without washing and stuck in the corner of my sock drawer. To Mother it would appear that the world was unchanged, that very little happened to me, just like last month and the one before that.

The thought of having to make small talk in an hour or so wasn't palatable. How could I fake some neutrality and talk about the weather after having finally understood why people were so crazy in their search for love? I wasn't even angry or pained anymore. It all just boiled down to the fact that I missed Ashlinn. People couldn't possibly get over things like this.

And so I sat on the couch and turned on the television in an attempt to appear as I usually would, only to find the *Singin' in the Rain* menu was still filling the screen. Without thinking, I hit Play, and once again the tears came, although they were courteous enough to hold out until after the opening number.

They were unobtrusive and only increased in quantity and not violence with every scene that passed. Mother returned before "If You," a fact for which I will never be grateful enough, and didn't even question the crying. It wasn't the first time she had found me in such a state, and she undoubtedly assumed I was upset about "missing" my auditions. Guilty much?

I suspected she never knew what to do, but her reaction wasn't bad. She sat down next to me and leaned my head against her chest where I cried softly until there was nothing left but heavy air and a dizzying amount of lonely tomorrows. When I looked up, the television was black.

That was a clockwork day. Emotionlessly, I floated through the house trying to appear normal while willing the night to come more quickly. That was my only chance. With day clothes on my body and freshly brushed teeth, I looked like a passable human. Now I just needed someone to appreciate it. What was Ashlinn doing at that moment? She could have been building castles in the minds of kindergarteners or reliving past loves with some old man in a nursing home. She was creating wonders while I pitied myself in my room. Maybe she was better off alone. Not that she'd ever actually be alone; she had Reeves.

The carnation was beyond dried up where it sat on my bedside table, and I feared it would crumble if I so much as breathed on the thing. I could always retrieve the dress to reminisce with, but that just seemed a bit too piney for my tastes. Instead, I lay on the floor, ignoring my bed, and stared at the ceiling. If I were a boy from some coming-of-age movie, I'd be tossing a baseball up and down endlessly. There were so many things to worry about—the results of my audition and Mother's mental state, to name just two—but the only cares flittering through my mind revolved around Ashlinn.

This could have gone on for who knows how long, but while in this pathetic horizontal state, my cell phone rang. And rang. It couldn't possibly have been anything important—there were no phones wherever Ashlinn was—but it just wouldn't stop. Probably some telemarketer.

With a groan, I sat up and flung my hand on the bedside table until I found the vibrating menace. Written across the screen in big white letters was *Ellie*.

Back into the fray.

"What?" I asked after picking up, my tone harsher than I'd like to admit.

"Whoa there, grumpster. Sorry if this is coitus interruptus or something. Jeez, I was just wondering if you and Ashlinn still wanted to be my cheering squad for the tattoo tomorrow."

Another thing I'd forgotten about. Great.

"Ashlinn isn't here anymore," I choked out the words like they were blocking my air.

"Where is she, then? In case you've already forgotten, I do have a car. We can pick her up."

"No, I mean she's gone away for good. I don't think I'm ever going to see her again."

"Oh no, hon. I'm so sorry. Do you want to talk about it? I can come over there right now, watch me. And I'll bring ice cream. That bitch."

"Please don't say that. I'm fine. It's not her fault. I don't like ice cream. Really, I'm okay."

The last thing I needed was for her to come over and begin grilling me for the details. I could just imagine the scenario: *Where did she go?* Ellie would ask.

Oh, I don't know. Just some sort of nether spheric layer of the universe where people walk through the minds of others and anything can be created from nothing. No big deal.

Ellie didn't seem like she believed a word of my excuse.

"Mhm. Well, you're not getting out of coming with me tomorrow in that case."

"But—"

"Nope. Don't even try it. You've seen the number of breakups I've dealt with. The best thing for you is to get out and watch your dearest friend Ellie make an astonishingly stupid decision that will most likely involve a lot of pain. Trust me. I'll pick you up at one tomorrow."

And with that she hung up. It looked like I wouldn't be stuck to my floor for the rest of eternity after all.

FIFTEEN

THAT NIGHT I fell asleep and woke up eight hours later. And nothing happened. There were no dreams of any sort, no nightmares or false awakenings. Just an empty spot in my memory. Ashlinn truly was gone.

I didn't tell Mother my plans for the day, not sure whether or not she'd agree with them. Even if she did, there was always a risk of her telling Ellie's parents for some obscure reason, and they had no idea this was even happening. She left for work at a much closer location than the previous week.

The morning was a blur of attempts at distracting myself, most of which only led to more thoughts of Ashlinn in a roundabout sort of way. I braided garden flowers into my hair as something to do, carefully weaving them through the strands. Looking beautiful on the outside might improve matters on the inside.

Ellie rolled up at one o'clock exactly, and I could have applauded her astuteness. She called to tell me of her arrival, blaming laziness for not bothering to come ring my doorbell, and spent the entire ride there talking excitedly of her plans for the tattoo and not once bringing up Ashlinn. I didn't give this girl nearly enough credit sometimes. Anyway, she told me how it was designed by a supercool guy named Ray with an amazingly impressive portfolio I really must look at when we got there.

Her appointment was at the only tattoo parlor in a twenty-mile radius. It was in a strip mall with a red brick storefront that added to its already intimidating appearance. She parked the car in the farthest spot possible, still not sure of her driving skills, and we headed toward the door.

"Aren't you frightened?" I asked. I wasn't even getting the tattoo and I was scared.

"Terrified," she responded with a laugh, "so let's get it over with."

A bell jangled when we walked in and a heavily pierced lady with black tied-up hair looked up from behind the counter. There were chairs on either side of the door and one was occupied by a bearded man who looked as if he might live in the place.

"Hello," Ellie said cheerily to the receptionist. "I have an appointment with Ray."

"ID."

The woman didn't even look up when she asked, and Ellie began rummaging through her bag with a weak smile, already getting flustered. When she finally dragged out her license, the receptionist took it and seemed to trust the validity, then held the plastic card back between two fingers.

"Go take a seat; he'll be with you in a sec. Here, fill out this paperwork while you're at it." She handed over a purple clipboard with a release form and a pen.

We went to the side of the room opposite the other customer, and I occupied myself by staring at the framed tattoo designs that adorned the walls. There were some pictures of generic lions and hearts, but also a few portraying swirls and pyramidal geometric shapes. I glanced over at what Ellie was busily filling out. She was answering questions about her age and any drugs she might be on, as well as consent to get the tattoo done at all. She warily marked off a box absolving the studio of any liability.

Impressively, her hands didn't seem to be shaking as she filled it out in bubbly penmanship. Mine would have been registering on the Richter scale in such a situation. She returned the forms to the woman, where they had a discussion ending with Ellie handing over fifty dollars. She made a big show of asking for the receipt, that being something she'd read online as a very important thing to do. Ellie took her seat yet again, fidgeting for a few moments before picking up a magazine to flip through. The waiting was making her increasingly tense. Finally she closed the magazine angrily in her lap then turned to me and stage-whispered, "Where's Ashlinn?"

I sputtered. "Do you really want to discuss this now? You're about to get a tattoo, dammit."

Our voices were much too loud for this conversation to be secret, but I tried to keep it down as much as possible.

"I've been really good about waiting this long, and I'm going to ask you eventually. It's either now or when I'm in the middle of having needles shoved in my skin."

"Or we can talk about it later. When we're done."

When I've thought of an excuse to avoid the conversation.

"Oh, Victoria," she said softly, "have you wanted to hang out recently? It's now or never. I was starting to like that girl. Where the hell is she and how can I help you get her back?"

"You can't help me. I'm sorry. Something terrible happened, and she had to go away. That's it."

My eyes were going glassy, so I kept them open as long as I could manage, staring at the floor and refusing to cry again. Ellie looked as if she was about to start pushing for information, but thankfully Ray emerged from the back just in time and interrupted us with a loose handshake and a grin.

"Good to see you again. Excited to get that devilish tattoo?"

And with that her mind found a new focus. "You know it. And I brought along moral support. Care to show her the design?"

"No problem. Come this way."

He beckoned us around a corner to a table where he pulled out a manila folder with the drawing inside. He proffered it to me.

"Whaddaya think?"

It was undoubtedly a devil, small but unmistakable, with two large ridges for horns and a spiked tail that made way for hoofed legs. The entire thing was one continuous black line, very simple and without color.

"Wow. It's something," I told him, handing back the artwork.

"It's perfect," Ellie breathed, and he smiled at the praise.

"I do try. This'll take no time at all. We can get started right away."

She looked nervous, and I could see her fingering the receipt in her pocket. I reached over and took her free hand, which seemed to shock the girl out of her fearful trance.

"Let's leave or let's do it. It's up to you."

She grabbed my hand tighter and looked up at Ray. "Let's do it."

"Great. We're going to do this in a private room considering it's your first time and you want it on a marginally private place. Your thigh, correct?"

She nodded, and he got up to cross the floor, which had benches and stations for those who didn't mind getting inked up in public view, and opened a black door on the other side. The area it led to had one padded bench that reminded me of the cots we used to have in the nurse's office at school. He gestured for Ellie to lie down on her front as I took a seat next to her.

"I'm going to push your shorts up a bit so I can get at where you want it, and then I'll shave that area and clean it with rubbing alcohol, okay?"

"Okay."

I liked him; he was talking her through every step of the process and his eyes never wandered. On the other hand, her eyes were closed the entire time Ray spent cleansing her thigh and shaving it with a disposable razor. After the shaving he cleaned it another time. I was probably the most uncomfortable out of the bunch, not knowing where to look. He continued the rundown.

"Now I'm going to put a transfer of the design on your skin. You'll be able to look in a mirror and see how pretty your tattoo is going to be and make sure you haven't made a rotten decision."

The transfer was like a temporary tattoo for grown-ups. He applied water first, then the image, and when the paper was removed a blueish-black outline of the Jersey Devil was left on her flesh. She climbed off the cot and contorted herself in front of a full-length mirror hanging on the door. Her elation upon seeing the image made it seem like she had never been frightened to begin with.

"This is so sick," she said optimistically to her reflection, and Ray and I were both quick to agree. While she appreciated the design that would soon be a permanent part of her, Ray began preparing the tattoo machine. He placed black ink in caps and inserted the appropriate needles, looking completely confident with the gun.

She lay down yet again and held out her hand for me to take, so I cradled it between my palms as he applied ointment to her thigh.

"I'm about to begin. After the first minute or two you'll get used to it, and it will hurt less. Are you absolutely sure you want to do this?"

"Of course. Get on with it."

He shrugged and began. When the needle first stroked her skin, she gasped and her fingers clenched against mine. I prayed that her thigh would stay still because the last thing anyone needs is a shaky tattoo or a long line permanently going across her leg.

"Say something distracting," she demanded tensely.

I panicked, and suddenly every anecdote or bad joke I could possibly tell vanished from my memory.

"Ummm…," I went, stalling for time as her hand held tightly to mine, "do you remember that time we broke into the old theater?"

She grunted in affirmation, so I decided this was a good topic to continue with.

"Daffodils were growing between the floorboards and there was all that mold. It smelled like absolute death, and the only beautiful things were the daffodils. We were what, in the fifth grade? And you said one of the most profound things."

"What was that?" she asked, beginning to ease up a bit.

"You told me how you hate daffodils because they're morbid. They stick around for a month making everything lemon-drop yellow, then die and get replaced by worse flowers. How the hell does an elementary schooler grasp the concept of beauty not being permanent? I remember being impressed. We were fearless that day."

"Wish I could be fearless now."

Ray interrupted to say that he was finished with about a quarter already so there wouldn't be too much left to endure. For a few minutes, the only sound in the room was the tattoo gun's mechanical stutter, but that was soon broken by Ellie, who was still in need of distraction.

"I'm going to ask you again, Victoria. Where is Ashlinn?"

"Nowhere we can visit. Not even The Hovercraft could take us."

"Have pity on me, girl. I'm weak and having needles shoved into my thigh. You're totally evading the question. You know, it's funny, I actually had a dream about your MIA girlfriend last night."

What?

At that I perked up, excited if not a bit jealous. Hopefully Ellie was too distracted to notice my desperation.

"What did you dream about?" I asked, squeezing the hand that had started to relax between mine.

"It was nothing. I think we were up in a tree, one that was covered in cherry blossoms. We were talking about you, actually, if I remember correctly. All good things. Who cares, though? It's always excruciating to hear other people's dreams. Although not as excruciating as having needles poked in your skin."

She shouted the last sentence over her shoulder at Ray, but he took it in stride and laughed.

"You chose to do this. We're almost done."

I desperately wanted to ask her to explain the dream more, to give details, and force her to remember everything. Did Ashlinn look like rainstorms? Was the cloak back? Was she sad? The biggest question of all is why Ellie got a visit while I remained ignored.

"Okay, so this is going to sound really odd," I began telling Ellie, although she might not have even been paying attention, "but if you ever dream of her again can you tell Ashlinn that I'm sorry."

She turned her head to the side and squinted at me.

"The two of you say some freaky things, you know that? I mean, if I remember, I will, but it's not like it even matters. I wish you would just explain this relationship to me, if that's what it is. Have you even broken up?"

I opened my mouth to answer but realized I had no idea. I had a negative amount of previous relationships to compare this one to.

"I'm not sure," I answered truthfully, then glanced over her back to investigate the tattoo's progress. The purple outline had been almost completely replaced by the inflamed black design.

Another silence stretched out in the room, except this one was uncomfortable. Thankfully, Ray was nearing the end.

"You're done," he announced, and Ellie's sigh of relief could have extinguished the Olympic torch. Before letting her up, he applied more ointment and a bandage, making her look wounded instead of artful, but it would be worth it once the gauze could be removed. That would take four hours at least. She received a pamphlet on aftercare and the deed was done. A lifelong decision that took under twenty minutes, and unlike the daffodils, beauty was now permanent. She gave Ray a hug, which he gladly returned, and we walked out the door to the parking lot.

"Shit," she exclaimed when we reached her car.

"What?"

"How am I gonna sit for this whole drive with a freaking open wound right under my ass?"

We stood behind The Hovercraft and stared at each other hopelessly, trying to will an answer to emerge.

"Can't you power through the pain? The drive isn't that long."

"It's sore and hurts like a bitch. It might still be bleeding for all I know. Can you drive?"

Silence.

"You know I don't do that."

"You took driver's ed sophomore year and have a license."

She wasn't taking no for an answer. Yes, I did have my license, but I never drove with it and had zero intention to. A part of me feared what losing another child to the road would do to my mother, but mainly I worried about causing an accident with collateral damage. I could turn some other girl out there into me. Even before losing Reeves and Dad, I was terrified of the videos in driver's ed, and after the accident, it took me months to even be a passenger. There were more reasons than could be counted on both hands as to why I shouldn't drive.

"I haven't got my license with me."

"So what? You won't get pulled over, and if we do, you can flash the officer mine and break out the girlish charm and tears."

"Even if I were to drive, you'd still have to sit down the whole time." I was getting desperate.

"Nah, I'll lie down in the back."

This plan was getting more insane by the second. She waved a dismissive hand at my incredulous expression.

"Oh, don't be like that. I trust you."

Reeves had trusted me. So had Ashlinn. That hadn't worked out particularly well, and no matter how many times I told myself neither of those endings was my fault, it just seemed too difficult to believe.

Right. I had to start letting go. This was becoming more of a study in self-love than anything.

"Fine, give me the keys," I relented. She tossed them to me, a wicked smile on her face, and climbed into the backseat as I ducked into the front. I closed my eyes, trying to bring the driver's ed textbook I practically memorized to the front of my mind, and pretended there was a driving instructor in the passenger seat. I'd be able to do this as long as there was no need to either parallel park or K-turn. Opening my eyes, I observed the surroundings. First, the mirrors had to be adjusted, then the seat belts secured.

"Seat belt?" I called back to Ellie.

"Can't. I'm lying on my front across the seats."

Looking back proved that indeed she was. Oh hell no.

"Don't care. Find a way."

She groaned but managed to wrap the belt from the middle seat I had occupied on our way to New York around her waist. I guess that was as good as it was going to get in the situation.

Next: keys, foot on brake, gear shift, steering wheel, gas. Seemed manageable.

I thought through every action before performing it, and soon enough the car was rumbling to life beneath my feet. I put the car into drive and released the brake, and we were crawling out of the parking lot and onto the road. With every honk of a road-rager behind us and every creep up to a red light, I felt myself finally letting go. This was danger without self-destruction.

SIXTEEN

ELLIE HAD to help me with directions at the start, but after we got closer to town, everything was familiar and I easily found her house. It looked like every other generic suburban home to grace America: a tan, two-storied affair with a neat lawn and white decorative windowpanes. Pulling up to her driveway made me realize our next issue.

"I didn't think this far in advance. I'm just going to walk home," I told her as I turned off the car and unbuckled my seat belt.

"Like hell you are," she responded, gingerly eradicating herself from the backseat. "I'm not letting you comfort me as I make a decision I'll probably regret in twenty years, then forcing you to walk home after graciously driving to ease my burning thigh. You're staying the night. If my skin feels less explosive in the morning, I'll drive you."

"It probably won't."

"Then we'll walk together. Now open the car door for me."

I did as she said and watched her gracelessly slide onto the driveway with her bottom lifted high in the air, then take far too long to stand. There was the ever-present urge to run home, blame dance and my mother, or even a debilitating illness, but things were tilting. I didn't want those factors to stop me; I just expected them to out of habit.

"Lead on," I told her after a second's hesitation. I reached for my phone to call Mother and explain how I was actually interacting with another human being. As it rang, Ellie half waddled up to the door, then picked up the mat with a wild, indiscreet flourish and found the key. We were inside before Mother even picked up.

Her hello was infused with so much terror over whatever catastrophe must have occurred for me to call, it was almost funny.

She would probably have been less surprised to hear news of me causing an impending apocalypse than that I was hanging out with someone. I told her I'd be staying the night at Ellie's without giving too much information away. Her enthusiasm over the friendship she believed me to be rekindling was a bit overboard, but at least she was actually expressing some sort of emotion.

"No, there will not be alcohol. Yes, I will call you in the morning. I'm sure she can lend me a toothbrush."

Ellie was laughing at the one side she could hear of my conversation, so I said good-bye and hung up as quickly as possible, still standing in the threshold. The inside of her house seemed unchanged from when I last saw it a year ago—or was it two? Dark stained hardwood floors and floral-print curtains framed every window.

"Is your room still in the basement?" I asked, remembering how cool I had always thought that was. She had an entire floor to herself, like a poor man's underground penthouse.

"Yeah, no reason to move. Let's go hide down there in case my parents show up soon and decide they want to do something disgusting like talk."

A wooden door gave way to narrow stairs with carpet obviously added as an afterthought. The walls were painted cinder blocks, and a single twin-size bed was pushed as far into the corner as it could go. There was a lot of empty floor space, yet an old tube television sat merely inches from the edge of the bed. A folding chair reclined in the center of the floor beneath a boa dangling from the ceiling next to a string of nonworking Christmas lights. Posters depicting artwork I was doubtful she had ever even seen were stuck to the walls with long lines of black electrical tape.

"It's changed," I said, surprised at the fact I was surprised.

"You can't stay fourteen forever. I had to get rid of the glitter eventually."

She flopped down face-first onto the bed, with one foot popped up in the air.

"Have I made a horrible decision?" she asked into her pillow.

"That's not for me to say."

I fell back into the folding chair, which topped the list as one of the most uncomfortable things my butt had ever come in contact with, and began to take the braids out of my hair.

"You know, I don't like this town all that much."

"Not many people do," I replied, not sure where this was going. If she was bringing up reasons why her tattoo might not have been the wisest decision, that would surely be one of them.

"I mean, the best thing about this place is its proximity to other places. We can get to New York, and there's the ocean and Atlantic City, but nothing is right here. I'd like to live somewhere that no one is ever bored."

"Well, you have choice pick of colleges with those grades of yours. Go to New York like I want to. Apply to NYU or Columbia or something."

I plucked the wilting flowers from my hair, surprised so many had stayed in, and lined them up on her floor.

She turned her head so she was no longer getting a mouthful of pillow whenever she spoke. "They're not far enough. I want to run away."

These admissions were surpassing whatever remained of my comfort level, but I was intrigued. We never spoke about anything personal, not anymore. We'd be delving into my sexual identity crisis soon at this rate.

"Run away?" I asked. "You just got a tattoo in dedication to the place you're currently bashing. If you're trying so hard to escape, why would you get a chunk of it on your thigh forever?"

"You already know my Jersey Devil story, which really was the initial reason, but I dunno." She stopped, thinking. "I guess I want the new people I'm going to meet to think I'm from somewhere worth remembering. Somewhere they'd have wanted to grow up. If they think I like it here, maybe I'll be able to start convincing myself too."

She paused again. "Besides, knowing I'm from New Jersey will make them less likely to mess with me." I could hear the smile in her voice at the end and snorted.

"You just need to act like yourself. If you do that, I think you're pretty safe from people messing with you no matter what they think of your hometown."

She began moving to turn over, then yelped in pain and lurched off the bed. "Goddammit!"

I tutted at her. "It is an open wound. You were bleeding what, twenty minutes ago?" She began reaching for the bandage, and I rushed to where she stood to smack her hand away.

"Did you even read the care instructions? He said four hours at least. Keep it on for a day. I doubt it's much to look at right now, anyways."

She pouted, but her anger was cut off by the click and slam of an opening door.

"Mom's home. I'll just go warn her that you're here."

"Wait," I said, stopping her as she headed toward the stairs. "Put on some pants. Loose ones."

Her eyes widened with the realization that she now had months of covering her thigh ahead of her. She couldn't afford to slip up like this.

"There is no way I'm getting jeans on over this. Help me find a longer skirt. One that'll reach my knees. Damn, this is going to be hell to hide for the next year."

We flung open her dresser, which was a mess of red and black fabric. Several skirts were folded or crumpled in the corners, making it look more like a wastepaper basket than anything. Each skirt was too short and would show the bandage from certain viewpoints. Clothes were being flung around like flags and thrown so that they billowed before reaching the floor, decorating the ground like a peddler's caravan. Finally we uncovered a dress that only reached midthigh in the front but tapered around to be nearly floor length in the back.

I turned my back to her as she painstakingly peeled off her clothes and donned the new outfit. It was nice, if a bit dressy for a summer afternoon.

"I'm decent," she called before jogging up the stairs. I headed up after her, watching the skirt flutter with each step like Ashlinn's cloak had when she walked down the beach, a memory I tried desperately to push away.

Ellie threw open the door at the top of the steps.

"Mom, Victoria's over."

"Really? I haven't seen her in ages." When I finally got out of the basement, her mother was there dropping a briefcase. She came over and gave me a hug.

"I hope everything's okay with you. It's nice to have you here." It sounded more like someone breaking the news to a toddler that their fish just went home to Jesus than anything. Pity would suffocate me in the end.

"Great to see you too," I lied. No one thinks to miss a friend's parents. She gave me a meek smile and walked toward the kitchen.

"Dinner's in an hour. I'm making spaghetti."

We filled the time between that moment and dinner with two episodes of *SVU* commentated obnoxiously by Ellie, who could find a flaw in any character. During the meal her mom spoke very little, and we all just stared down into our plates of pasta. I was well acquainted with this form of "family dinner." The scraping of forks against china punctuated an invisible conversation Ellie seemed to be engaged in with her mother. It was less effort to just ignore the whole thing than to try and interpret their eyebrow raises and fleeting hand gestures. I never asked where her father was.

After dinner Ellie rescued a tub of ice cream from the freezer for herself and tossed me a bag of Twizzlers I had little intention of actually eating.

"Truth or Dare. Truth or Dare," she chanted as we headed back downstairs.

"What?"

"It's a slumber party. We have to play truth or dare."

After closing the door carefully behind us and returning to the bed, she attempted to lie on her front again but realized that position wasn't suitable for eating ice cream and modified the situation. After pulling over the folding chair, Ellie inserted herself face-first through the back so that her arms dangled toward the ground, and propped her feet up on the mattress. Uncomfortable but effective.

"You first," she said, pointing at me with her spoon where I sat crisscrossed before her on the floor. "Truth or dare?"

"Dare."

"No, I think you want truth."

"Okay, then, truth."

"What the hell was that whole Ashlinn affair? Explain in detail, citations not necessary. Go."

As if I couldn't see that one coming. "I change my mind. Give me my dare back."

Ellie smirked at me. "No can do. Might as well get it over with, 'cause you know I'm going to torture you about this whenever we see each other until you give up. I am damn persistent and endlessly stubborn."

Lord knows that's the truth. My options were diminishing, and Ellie already suspected that something was off about the relationship. Time to see what she'd be willing to believe; hopefully there wouldn't be a great need to invent a European family Ashlinn had to visit or any other lies. Like I had told Ashlinn, I leave the storytelling and creativity to others.

It seemed safe to start with the basics, gain a jumping-off point to figure out how much could be revealed. "What do you believe in, Ellie?"

"Hey, it's my turn to ask questions. Don't try and change the subject."

"I know. We're getting to my answer; just help me."

"Well, whaddaya mean? Like, Santa and shit? Or are we talking some sort of existential, what-values-do-you-hold-dear kinda business?"

"Anything. Supernatural creatures, God. You have the Jersey Devil on your thigh…. That must mean something."

She placed her carton of ice cream on the floor and allowed her head to dangle down, eyes closed in thought. "This is deep, man. I guess I believe in it all. I mean, I don't want to, but I can't help it. God, you said? Hell, I don't want to believe in the dude, but it's hard not to sometimes."

"Why don't you want to believe in God?" As someone who could never work up any faith of my own, it seemed like a nice thing to have. A sort of insurance policy for the afterlife just in case there was an actual possibility of being damned.

"Too much pressure. They tell us this guy has power over everything that ever is or was. Well, that means he planned for us to happen, right? This omnipresent being caused the Ice Age and sent the asteroid that destroyed the dinosaurs. What if he killed off the mammoths to make way for us? He needed room for the humans and got rid of 'em. That's a lot to live up to, my friend. I'm not sure if my existence justifies losing the mammoths."

Irritatingly erudite seemed like her default setting. "And where do you think dreams come from?" I asked, feeling like I was inching over a frozen lake that had just begun to crackle.

"I don't know. They come from that big squashy thing called your brain."

We needed more whimsical thinking and less of that AP, honor roll, Ivy League logic. The worst part is that what she said was true. There was just more at play than that.

"What if I were to tell you that Ashlinn's gone away to some place as intangible as where you get your dreams from?"

She lifted her head and watched as I rubbed my fingers repetitively along the hem of my dress. "Like the Arctic? Or Narnia? Ooh, maybe the magical land of, what did you guys say you were?" She paused for a moment and then sneered. "Oh right, asexuals."

When people talked about breaking points, generally they acted like it was something you were aware of, something being built up to. Counting the straws in preparation for one to break the camel's back. That wasn't how it worked for me. There was no bubbling up, just a sudden switch.

"What the hell do you have against asexuality?" I cried, probably showing more emotion than Ellie was used to ever seeing from me, my hands flying wildly and accidentally whacking the bag of Twizzlers across her floor. "You act so damn accepting. Why can't you accept this?"

"Because it doesn't make any sense, and I'd never even heard of it before you brought it up. I even tried looking it up, and I gotta tell you that I'm still completely baffled. You're just confused.

Don't you think everyone would know about this if it existed? Liking sex is a good thing."

I wanted nothing more than to storm out of there. To scream at her about how wrong she was and angst over the ignorance of others. But there was something in her words that I recognized, something I had once thought myself.

"The world is learning. Do you honestly think you know everything that's out there? Look, whether you acknowledge that this is how I am or not, it isn't going to change the truth."

"But sex is so nice. You've never even had sex, have you? You can't say you don't like something you don't understand. Maybe that's why Ashlinn left."

This was excruciating.

"I don't see how that's any of your business. I doubt you go around grilling every gay boy on the street about his sex life just to make super sure he isn't heterosexual. Look, you're straight."

"Indeed I am," Ellie drawled out, her ice cream now deliquescing where it sat on the floor.

"And when did you figure that out?"

"S'pose I've always known. Guess in the sixth grade when I wanted to unwrap Clayton Hino instead of his Oreos was the true kicker."

"And how do you know you're straight if you've never slept with a girl?"

"Because I'm not gay. It's that easy. I don't find girls attractive like that."

Understanding seemed to be growing in Ellie with that statement. She raised an eyebrow at me.

"I think you're starting to catch on," I told her proudly, crawling over to save the Twizzlers. "That's the way I feel about sex with anyone."

"Okay, but you were totally in a relationship with a girl."

"Yeah. I liked her. I still do. It was romantic."

"And you never had sex?"

"Nope."

"And you were okay with that? Both of you?"

"Yup. It's literally that easy."

"Hmmm...." Ellie was thinking over the words. "I'm not going to pretend to understand but I'm getting there. Whatever makes you happy, I suppose. You deserve that much by now." She cleared her throat and picked up the ice cream again. "Sorry about the shouting," she mumbled.

"Try to not do it again."

"I still don't know what happened to your arm candy. If your plan was to distract me, it succeeded."

"You've already gotten enough emotional admissions out of me for one day. Can't we deal with this later? She's gone."

Ellie must have felt guilty because she just nodded and agreed. We had no more in-depth girl conversations that night. Instead she rolled out of her chair/bed hammock and began prepping for the night. Every winter blanket that her mother stored in the basement was thrown onto the floor next to her bed for me to mold into a sleeping bag of some sort. Lying all the way on the floor, the only part of Ellie I could see was her foot in the air.

She was more somber than usual as we tried to resume our roles as average teenage friends, ones I'm not sure we ever filled to begin with. We watched the *SVU* marathon for hours, complaining about how they were only showing recent episodes. It must have been past two in the morning when she convinced me to climb to the top of her stairs and shut out all the lights, and with "criminal offenses considered especially heinous" playing in the background, I drifted off to sleep.

SEVENTEEN

ON THE floor in the basement of a house I only pretended to be comfortable in, a carnival was moving in slow motion through my head. A massive tent stretched out around me, tinting the light pink as it filtered through red stripes. The makings of an elaborate circus act were being arranged directly beneath the pointed center. Sluggish elephants and trapeze artists in diamond-print harlequin spandex inched along tightropes at a pace so slow it would be impossible to imitate. Striped hoops stood upright on the dirt floor and the remnants of what seemed to be a juggling act were littered around the bases they stood on.

There were rows and rows of children watching everything, frozen in place with enraptured expressions and eyes locked on the action. No one towered over them. This world was muted, but I didn't notice until a sound was finally made in contrast.

"I've missed you," said a low voice from over my shoulder. A voice that was foggy and whimsical, full of memory.

Ashlinn.

I found myself flat on my back before she even got the second word out, and she walked around to stand over me, then offered a hand to help me up. Still, I did not move from the ground.

"Are you really there?" I whispered.

She nodded, seeming on edge, like a teenager from a caffeine-free family after their first Starbucks. Undoubtedly she had something urgent to say or do, but I was too busy staring to bother asking. Beginning with the legs I was eye level with, I began scanning her body. The dusky cloak had returned as well as the umbrella. Her eyes were the last thing I met mine with, and there was an electric current in hers. How was this possible?

She left me. How could she visit Ellie and not me.

A part of me wanted her to feel a tiny bit guilty, even though there was little blame and we needed to share it. Instead I just apologized. If anyone needed to absolve themselves of guilt, it was me.

"I am so sorry," I croaked out, and meant every word more than a lot of things I'd spoken before.

She sat on her knees, then pulled me into a hug. My arms were still limp at my sides, so it was less of an embrace and more having my face crushed into her chest as I attempted to force my sense of smell to begin functioning through sheer willpower.

"It wasn't your fault. None of it was your fault."

She kept repeating those words like a mantra, and I absorbed them willingly, yearning to believe everything.

When she began to pull back, I lifted my arms to grab her, refusing to be released.

"Where have you been?" I asked, the first of many questions I didn't want to ruin the moment with but felt compelled to ask. Her cloak was hardly tangible beneath my fingers, yet I still rubbed her back.

"Doing what I've always done. Everything has returned to normal. Hopefully you've seen, and it's all for the best. People are dreaming of pleasant things as well as the bad."

"Except for me," I whispered with a poorly disguised note of malice.

"Except for you. I haven't been strong enough to visit you, knowing I couldn't let you see I was there controlling your fantasies, but I did strike a deal with Semira. She shouldn't bother you too much anymore. It's an apology. You see, if I don't give you good dreams, it doesn't matter if she undoes the nightmares because there is still a balance. Those vile images will never haunt you again."

Now I did pull back, although I kept my hands on her airy wrists.

"I'll take those ugly things if I can still see you. Semira is sick, and I do not mean that in the good way. I want you to feel comfortable around me and now I'm not sure how you possibly could. I would never do those things we saw in the mirrors. I can't even imagine it."

"I know."

"Then," I began meekly, staring at her dress and not her eyes, "where have you been? I think I could live with a lifetime of only seeing you when I'm asleep if you could still stay a part of my life."

"And what kind of life would that be? One where reality seems less important than the time you spend unconscious? You could get hooked on sleeping pills. Victoria, you deserve a life like everyone else and the ability to chase more dreams than the ones locked away in your head. I let you go because I love you, and I'm trying to not be selfish anymore."

If this was her idea of a breakup note, I couldn't handle it. In my eyes she was masking her abandonment as care. Not to mention this was the second time she had given me the gift of that four-lettered L-word while I still hadn't returned the favor, but this time I couldn't accept it sweetly.

"There's no need to coddle me. Shockingly enough, I am capable of chasing both you and my dreams, two things that have become intertwined in more ways than one. Let me watch out for myself. Obviously you've been trying, but that ridiculous plan of yours to avoid me hasn't been working out too hot considering you're here in my dream."

"That's the thing," she stated, "this isn't your dream."

I looked around at the fantastical setting. There was an elephant standing on its front legs not eight feet from where we were pretzeled together on the floor.

"What is it? This sure as hell isn't reality."

"This is your brother's dream."

Her gaze on me was unwavering and all my muscles locked in place.

"What?" I asked, no louder than one would speak in a silent church.

"I may have figured out a compromise, a way we can be together."

Her words were thrilling, but I was still in too much shock for them to truly sink in. She continued.

"But your brother comes into it. Reeves has a big decision, and he asked to speak to you before making it. I beckoned you to this world I created for him, much in the way I brought Semira to your dream, although the consequences of the nightmares she created were probably much more troublesome than this will prove to be."

"Where is my brother? What does he have to do with this?"

Ashlinn stood up. She brushed off the front of her dress although it was perfectly clean and shook her umbrella before positioning it higher up on her arm, which she then stretched down to help me up.

"I'll take you to him now," she said as I accepted her hand.

The butterflies in my stomach were not from her touch but the thought of seeing Reeves. The concept was so intimidating I almost forgot to be excited. What if he was disappointed in me? He could be different from how I remembered; seeing him in the hospital had caused enough reevaluation of the last year as it was.

Ashlinn and I walked past the continual lines of motionless children when I noticed movement among their frozen faces. Several rows down, all the way in the front, a brown-haired head was bobbing on a bench. I released Ashlinn's hand to sprint toward my brother. It could be no one else.

The distance between us shrank at a greater pace than what I was running at, and soon I was on my knees in front of where he was sitting. His eyes were actually open. I placed my hands on his shoulders.

"Oh my God."

He looked angelic. In the hospital his freckles had faded, but now they blossomed all over his skin in constellation patterns. Reeves's hair was an absolute mess, sticking off his head in every direction, and he was grinning like there was nothing else he'd rather be doing than watch me fall apart at his feet.

"Hey, sis," he said loudly. Actually, it may have been a normal volume, but to my ears his voice was thunderous. My arms were shaking where they lay on his shoulders and my heart was on the verge of vibrating right out of the rib cage it was trapped inside.

"I have missed you. So much."

I had told Ashlinn the same thing, but this held a completely different meaning. His smile grew into the one he wore whenever I'd trip across the floor or spill something. At this moment I was willing to take any joy at my own expense if it meant he would keep grinning. I had forgotten how pronounced his dimples became when truly overjoyed, like that time he got a participation trophy for baseball. Dad told him it meant he was voted best player, and Reeves spoke of nothing else for days.

"I've missed you too. An accident, huh? And Dad's dead? It doesn't seem real. I'm almost happy I can't remember it. Not really, though, because the whole thing has been driving me nuts. It must've been superhard for you guys, seriously, but Ashlinn has told me lots of things, and it's time to let go," he said, and I began to remove my hands from his shoulders. He just shook his head.

"Not literally. I mean you and Mom need to move on. So do I. Ashlinn's tried to explain things to me, but I'm more than a little mixed up about this whole situation. Still, she's been really nice. When I think about Dad and get upset, she always seems to be there."

He nodded in her direction. She was standing a good distance from us, pretending to be preoccupied by a lady on stilts slowly raising one leg.

"She really does love you," he continued conspiratorially. "I almost got tired of hearing about how fantastic and interesting you are all the time. It's kinda gross."

Now why couldn't Ellie be more like that? His perception of our "grossness" had nothing to do with our sexualities—I doubt he even cared we were both girls—but instead because my girlfriend thought I was great.

I finally spoke to him again. "At least you haven't been lonely. I'm really happy about that. From the outside it doesn't look like you're having the most interesting time."

"Is it bad?" he asked, losing the joyful attitude.

"What?"

"Me. In the coma. How do I look?"

Oh, you know, half-dead and ghostlike. Immobile. It breaks Mother's heart.

"It looks like you're sleeping, that's all."

That smile returned.

"Good. I might forget that soon, but it's nice to know. Only the important things seem to stick in my memory. For example," he began, as if reciting vocab words, "I know I'm in a coma and that I love you and Mom and Dad. But Dad is dead and I'm allowed to be sad about it. I know that Ashlinn is my closest friend. Everything's been sort of—" He paused, searching for a word, then snapped his fingers when he found it. "—gooey. This dreaming is a bit strange for me, but she says there's a way I can un-goo everything and move on. If I do it, you two will be able to spend your lives together and do coupley stuff."

There was no hint of a lie in his eyes, and God knows I'd be good at detecting that from our childhood together.

"How?" I asked, urging him to continue. "I'll do whatever it is."

"You won't have to do anything from the sound of it. See, there's always gotta be someone to make the good dreams. When Ashlinn became human everything was dark for me, and apparently the rest of the world wasn't having a much better time. There's nothing that says the person who breaks into people's minds has to be your girlfriend. We can have a sand*man* instead, just like the fairy tale."

"Wait, what are you saying?" I asked warily, picking those words with care.

"I can do it." He lit up as he spoke, his body rigid with excitement. "I can take over for Ashlinn. She'll make me a cloak and train me and when we're through, I don't have to be trapped in this head of mine any longer. I'll be able to jump from dream to dream and eavesdrop on everyone's secrets."

I wanted to speak, but there were no words to say, not that I would have been able to get them out in the monologue he was still continuing.

"I'll make the best dreams ever for the both of you, and for Mom too."

As he began to list off the things he expected to find in the heads of others, I looked at Ashlinn over my shoulder. When she caught my eye I beckoned to her. His happiness was becoming contagious, but I didn't want to believe everything for fear of getting my hopes up and having it all turn out to be impossible.

"Is what he's saying true?" I asked when she appeared at my side.

"Yes, but there's a side effect."

That was never a good sign. This was turning into a good news/ bad news situation, and I gulped in anticipation.

"Side effect?"

Reeves was quiet now, watching the exchange with a hopeful expression still plastered on his face.

"He can't stay in the coma."

"Well, I don't think he can get out of it. Believe me, I've wanted nothing more for the past year."

"No, he can't get out of it." She was speaking like someone attempting to placate a dog they just kicked. "Reeves's body will die if he does this."

"No!" I shouted. "It would destroy my mother if he died. He's here right now, and he's not dead." I looked back and forth between them anxiously. "Can't you give him some of your magical voodoo crap now and let us carry on as is?"

"There's a reason I had to pick between my human and dream forms. Living people are not free to walk between dreams. Imagine all the messes you guys would get into if that were possible. I have that freedom, and the ability to bring others along, but only those of us without physical forms for our minds to cling to can do such things."

Reeves touched my arm, and although his grasp was just as nonexistent as Ashlinn's, it managed to get my attention.

"I don't want anyone to waste their lives sitting next to a hospital bed, and I don't want to be lying in one all that much either. I know you said Mom's doing okay, but it can't be all that easy." I hadn't heard a voice so uncertain since the accident.

"I don't want to go to another funeral."

My throat felt as if it were stuffed with cotton balls. Those words made me feel selfish, but they were the truth. Reeves didn't understand how Dad's funeral had been surreal; it was like an out-of-body experience, and I wanted to tear at my flesh just so I'd have something real to blame the pain on. It wasn't an event I cared to repeat, and Reeves didn't even know I'd had to deal with that already. They say I stood and stared at my father's bolted-shut casket until I was dragged away.

Reeves was looking at me imploringly, with large, childish eyes, and I hated that this was my decision to make.

"You can't possibly want to die. Aren't you frightened?"

"No. It won't be death, not really. If anything, it's immortality. Like a superpower."

"Will you be happier than you are now?"

"Yes." There was no hesitation.

"Will I ever see you?"

"Definitely."

Well, that's something. I had never expected to see him again in this lifetime. If anything, this would only improve our relationship, but I couldn't get past the thought of his lungs giving up and him lying there, cold and unmoving. Dad devoid of life was one thing; this was another. Undoubtedly both images would never be erased from my memory, and on top of it all, it just seemed so unfair to Mother. She would never know that he wasn't truly dead.

No. It was time for me to dabble in not being selfish, to continue following Ashlinn's lead and do what would make my brother happiest. God knows he deserved it.

"It's your life. You have my blessing to try and be happy. You know how to make your own decisions."

He threw his arms around me in triumph and his expression must have been awfully entertaining judging by Ashlinn's laughter behind me.

"Thank you," he whispered in my ear before releasing me so that my girlfriend could come over and get her share of the hugs.

"We can be together now," she said with wonder in her eyes. In my worry about Reeves's well-being, I had actually forgotten about the true motivation for all this. What a daunting, dizzying concept. This was something I wanted but was in no way prepared for. My thoughts were scattered like birdseed.

"There's so much I have to show you about being human. We can wait for my acceptance letter together."

"Have you ever had ice cream?" Reeves asked her, hopping up and down in his seat.

She shook her head no, but did so in such an excited fashion that the gesture seemed positive.

"You must. Take her to get ice cream right away, Victoria," he demanded with absolute authority, and I agreed that would be on the top of our to-do list.

"You can come to school with me, but I'm not sure if you want to." My head was whirling with ideas that seemed necessary to discuss at the time. "Where are you going to stay? This is permanent, isn't it?" I trailed off. This was too much to absorb.

She pulled me back into the hug, the impact of which was dulled by Reeves's disgusted noises in the background.

"We'll figure it out. And before that, I'll make sure to pop into the dreams of a few of those admissions officers."

Ashlinn winked, and whatever part of me would have admonished her for the sneakiness of it all was crushed by the need for everything to keep going right. It seemed like the world was starting to allow my elation, and an acceptance letter would help all of us in the long run. I giggled and continued to rejoice.

"Come on, Ashlinn," Reeves said, exasperated. "I wanna start learning now."

She turned to him, the pink light shining over one side of her face.

"Patience, okay? We'll start when she wakes up. You won't have too much longer to wait by the looks of things."

"When will I get to see you again?" I asked. Hopefully she'd be able to become human sooner rather than later.

"Oh, we'll take a few strolls through your subconscious in the coming days, I'm sure. Not too positive how long his training will take on your timescale, but it'll give you something to look forward to."

If I could wait for a garden to grow, then I could sure as hell wait for this.

"I'll be counting down every second. Visit me. You also," I said, pointing to my brother. "And why don't you think about popping around Mother's dreams sometime? She could use it." Maybe that would ease her pain slightly.

"Yes, ma'am," he replied with a little mock salute.

The last image I could recall of that dream involved Reeves and Ashlinn, hand in hand, walking out the front flap of the circus tent. I awoke in a different world.

EIGHTEEN

ELLIE'S BASEMENT was closing in around me. In the dark the wooden beams of her unfinished ceiling with screws protruding at every angle seemed terrifying. At first I couldn't figure out where I was.

I was in a strange place, and soon Ashlinn would be returning. How's that for a morning?

"Holy shit," I whispered, and a head swung over the bed next to me.

"I'll say" came Ellie's voice, and I screamed. She was partially illuminated by the light of her cell phone. "Whoa, I know I'm not much to look at in the morning, but my parents will think I'm murdering you."

"Sorry, I was just a bit disoriented." I couldn't wipe the smile off my face. That dream had truly just happened and every other issue seemed minuscule in comparison to such a tremendous win.

"And stupidly happy it would appear."

"Yeah, I am. Good dream, I guess. Have you been up long?" I asked, using my elbows to sit up. The small slit-like windows running around the top edge of her basement walls let in hardly any light, not enough to determine the time of day by.

"Nah, just about a half an hour. It's before nine. You're easy in comparison to some of the girls from my chem class. They come over and sleep 'til one, and I'm just stuck lying here as my phone dies from too much Pac-Man."

She got out of bed, stumbling over me in the process. After some shouts of pain from both of us, she managed to leap over the roadblock of my body and use her phone as a dim flashlight to climb the stairs and turn the actual lights on. At least this time she didn't ask me to do it. The fluorescent lights made me blink blearily as I ran my hands through my hair. Ellie's was spiked every which way, but then again, she does that on purpose.

"We can probably take the bandage off now," I said, trying to divert her from my excitement as she wandered back over to my pile of blankets. There was so much to think about, but this was not the place.

"Go for it."

She turned to stand in front of me, expecting me to do the honors. I kneeled behind her and started to take the tape away.

"Careful."

"Sorry, can't help you much there."

I tried to peel it off more slowly as Ellie twitched.

"It hurts," she whined.

"You got a freaking tattoo, and now you're complaining about the tape. Unbelievable." And with that I just got it over with and tore off the bandage. Ellie gasped like someone had poured ice water over her head and turned back to me.

"Why you little—"

"It looks amazing," I exclaimed. "Give me your phone. I'll show you a picture."

The news that this permanent work of art wasn't dreadful seemed to excite her enough, and she handed me her cell. The picture was a bit shaky, and the results were still inflamed, but she might as well have been looking at the Sistine Chapel with her reaction.

"This was the best decision ever. Do you think my parents would catch on if I set this as my screensaver? I am the sexiest bitch alive. I swear to God I'm going to tattoo every inch of my body."

"Whoa there. Let's get you a job first, okay?"

"We'll see."

"Does it hurt?" I asked. The skin was still angrily red.

"Not nearly as bad. I'll totally be able to drive you home. Might as well get going."

I changed back into my clothes from the day before, wondering why I had even bothered to snatch her pajamas to start with, and we left after a breakfast of cereal and Pepsi. Ellie didn't bother to put on normal clothes, just shoes because she didn't trust her ability to work the pedals in slippers or barefoot, and we drove the few miles to my house.

"See you soon," Ellie told me as I was getting out of her car.

"Yeah, you probably will."

"And look, I'm sorry about what I said last night."

Wouldn't she be surprised when Ashlinn came back. Hopefully she'd go easy on the girl.

I nodded and waved good-bye. She drove off, and I gave thanks for the fact that she hadn't played "Green Tambourine" once in the past two days.

Mother was home and let me in the house. She was pulling her sweater tightly around her form, yet I dragged her into a hug anyway. That was new, and she tried to stifle her surprise.

Waiting for Ashlinn made every day cheerier and full of anticipation. I practiced pirouettes on my hardwood floor as plans of what to do with her flitted through my mind. At night she no longer shied away from my dreams although our "dates" were infrequent due to her need to train Reeves.

One morning I came downstairs to Mother holding her mug at the kitchen table, and she smiled into it. That was something I hadn't seen in quite some time. I could guess the reason for her near-joy.

"Good morning. You seem cheery."

I noticed something a bit more lifelike in her eyes.

"You know what? I almost am. Last night I had a dream about Reeves, and it wasn't a bad one. Not about the crash or anything, like usual." She ran her fingers up and down the mug's handle. "He just stood there, looking so perfect and exactly how he always had. I feel like I should be upset, but I don't know. I saw my boy again, and he was completely okay."

I walked over and put my hand on her shoulder. "My dreams about him are starting to get better too. I think we're going to be okay ourselves."

And in that moment, we definitely were.

The next time Reeves showed up in my dreams, I thanked him for visiting her. He came all by himself that night, and the pride in his own abilities after doing so was beyond endearing.

Other nights he and Ashlinn built corn mazes and tree forts and symphony halls in my head. Sometimes he seemed a bit glum, and I had to assume it was because of Dad. There were more good-byes, although unnecessary, and a little over a week later, I met them both in a dream together.

We were standing at the edge of a forested cliff, looking over a waterfall. Cornflower-blue water was pouring to the ground like a rain of gemstones, turning to mist before hitting the distant rocks. Reeves was at the edge, wearing a suit of stars and deep blue midnights with a stiff white umbrella at his side. They were a handsome pair, and he looked older. It made the fact I'd never see him truly age that much more despairing.

"Look at you," I said, feeling almost maternal over the boy, like it was his first day of kindergarten and I wasn't ready to send him out into the cruel world.

"I know. They should parade me down a runway like this."

Better than being sent to a grave. The next suit I see him in won't be like this.

"I'm scared," I whispered, and Ashlinn left his side to wrap an arm around my shoulders.

"But you're also brave. Be there for your mother. We'll be looking out for you."

The splashing water drowned out any bird call or rustling leaves, yet I could hear her voice perfectly.

"Do you trust me?" she asked, as if the answer weren't obvious.

"More than anything."

Ashlinn took my hand in hers and began backing up toward the edge of the cliff. I assumed she would stop before reaching the brink, but instead she kept pulling me along before blindly teetering back and stepping off.

There was no trepidation or shock in her eyes the whole time, as we fell together. The air was rushing around like a million hair dryers set on high, and there was no sight or sound. The only feeling was the anchors of her hands in mine.

And before we could hit the ground, Ashlinn caught me.

NINETEEN

THREE DAYS passed and ended with a funeral. I had procrastinated on preparing for Reeves's death, not that there was much anyone could do to brace themselves for mortality, and when I found myself sitting on my bedroom floor after the news came from Mother, it felt like all my insides had been scraped out. I was hollow.

When Dad died I had wept for days, extending into long months, but now I was floating. Like an out-of-body experience. Someone needed to reassure me that everything was, in fact, okay, because it sure didn't feel that way. Mother's universe had collapsed, and that was reason enough to grieve.

The doctors said Reeves's heart just gave out, that they didn't know what went wrong. There wasn't any sign of secondary infection. I held my mother on the couch through violent tears, and her body was a tortured animal in my arms. She must have had such different expectations for the way her life would turn out; whatever dreams had been spun for her in her youth probably held such promise, but this was where she ended up. One lost year starting with becoming a widow and ending with losing a son. There would be no coming back from this, and I was little comfort in my own broken state. Together, perhaps, we'd make a presentable human and pick up each other's pieces, as shattered and in need of rearranging as they were.

The funeral came quickly. I'm not sure why I expected seeing him laid out in that setting to not be all that different from viewing his comatose form, because they were in no way alike. Someone had obviously been paid rather well to groom him and try to restore something lifelike to his skin.

They had failed.

Ellie came with her mother, who signed the guest book for both of them, and all three of us were wearing the exact same outfits we had worn to Dad's funeral last year. Like every other person who came, old school friends of Reeves, distant relatives, and so on, Ellie told me how profoundly sorry she was with glistening, pink eyes. Her mouth was as straight as the lines going up the back of her black tights, and she might have been more beside herself than I was.

As the pastor spoke in mellow tones about Reeves being in a better place, I looked up toward the ceiling, finally grateful, wondering if anyone realized how true those words were. Not that I was completely positive of their validity, a part of me still wondering if the whole thing had been a delusion. Some sort of sick way to cope with losing both him and Ashlinn, but there was no way my imagination could have made up such a perfect recreation of my brother. Even if I never saw him in person again, I could be happy knowing he was free.

No one slept that night. Or, at least, no one in my house. In her bedroom Mother was trying to muffle her sobs but the sharp intakes of breath still drifted down the hall. A better daughter might have gone in there to comfort her, but there was nothing to say. Some unimaginable pains have to be endured alone. I just feared for her sanity after I headed off to college. The wounds might never heal, but that doesn't mean we'd stop putting Band-Aids on top, and I wasn't sure if she could do that alone.

The hours ticked by, and my ceiling got less exciting by the second, so I crawled over to my closet with a flashlight, trying to avoid the creaky parts of my floor, and pulled out the book of fairy tales. It was splayed open like a squashed insect in the corner with my license. Many of the pages were bent in on themselves. Sitting in the doorway to our kingdom, I opened to the tale of the sandman and read it, imagining my brother as the main character. He had been hearing his own life story without even realizing it. Now that's celebrity preceding someone to the extreme.

That was how I spent the hours after my brother was lowered into the ground: reading words meant for children and dabbling in being an insomniac.

I never did sleep that night, but my mother managed to drift off sometime, probably on top of a soaked pillow. Around midnight the audible sobbing stopped, but who knows how much longer she lay awake. Maybe some comfort was waiting in her dreams, though.

The next morning as she slept off a bit of her grief, I tiptoed past her door and headed downstairs to the kitchen for breakfast. Our milk had expired the previous day, so I poured cereal and sat down with it dry, not really intending to eat anything but satisfied to have gone through the motions of normality. My unwatered garden watched as I pretended to eat, and I stared back exhaustedly. It desperately needed to be tended to.

Just as I considered going outside to try and resurrect the carnations, my cell phone began ringing on the table.

Ellie.

I pressed the green button to talk.

"What?" I hissed angrily, hoping the noise hadn't woken Mother. Did this girl realize what we were dealing with? She had been at the funeral not twenty hours before.

"Your girlfriend is in my fucking house! I think she broke into my room. I mean, sorry about the timing, but this isn't cool." She sounded completely out of her mind and was breathing like she was calling from a treadmill.

Holy crap.

"Don't call the police," I rushed to say as I ran to grab some paper and my purse. Ashlinn was here.

"That's all you have to say? Don't call the fucking police? Of course I didn't call them. I called you, dammit. Why the hell did you say that? Has she been on the run or something? Holy crap, you dated a murderer. She runs a drug cartel."

"No she doesn't, I promise. Where is she?" I uncapped the pen and began to write a note to Mother.

"In my bedroom. She was standing at the end of my bed wearing nothing but my goddamn sweater and saying how there's an explanation blah blah blah. I got out of there and locked the door as quick as I could. You are damn lucky my parents are heavy sleepers and my room is in the basement."

With the phone jammed between my face and shoulder, I scrawled how I was going to Ellie's but prayed that Mother wouldn't wake up before my return. To find one child missing the day after the other's funeral was beyond my imagining, but there was no time to think up a better plan. Ashlinn was human, Ellie was a catastrophe, and I was wasting moments. I left the paper on the kitchen table and went out the front door, which I opened so slowly it barely creaked. The second it was shut, I broke into a sprint down the sidewalk.

"I'm on my way now but can't guarantee how fast I'll be able to run this. Don't worry, she wasn't really breaking and entering." *I hope. What was Ashlinn trying to pull here?* "You can go back into your room."

"No way, not until you're here. This kind of shit doesn't happen every day. I could have easily thrown my lamp at her and caused major damage. I thought you said she was gone!"

"Yeah, well, apparently she's back now. I thought it might happen soon but not like this. Sorry."

"Oh are you? Well, if you know so much, mind telling me why the hell your long-lost girlfriend is half-naked in my bedroom at seven in the morning?" Ellie was shouting, and I worried about her parents. She had said they were heavy sleepers, but this made it seem like they could sleep through a brass band marching. If only I could give her an honest answer for all this, but that idea had fizzled and died the last time I tried it.

Wait, I thought back to what Ellie just said, *half-naked?* Ashlinn was going to have so much explaining to do when I got there.

After Ellie was an appropriate distance away, of course.

I guess warning me she was about to pull this stunt would have made things too easy.

"What were you dreaming of?" I asked, turning the corner. Empty roads made the run easier not only because there was no waiting at intersections, but also because it meant no one would think I'd gone off the deep end and call the police. It was just a matter of not tripping over the mountainous cracks in our sidewalk.

"How the hell do you know I was dreaming? This can't be relevant."

"Could be."

"I was dreaming of her, and now I know why! I swear she's become a recurring nightmare or something. We were talking about you, thanks a lot, on the Golden Gate Bridge, of all places. There were seagulls. It really shouldn't be all that shocking that I dreamed of someone who was in the same goddamn room as me. Are you almost here? There's no noise coming from down there, and it's freaking me out."

"Less than a minute away. I'm serious, she isn't some sort of wild animal you have to listen up at the door for. You really can talk to her; you've done it before."

Her driveway came into view, and I used the last of my energy running double time toward it. My forehead and chin were turning tacky with sweat.

"I'm gonna wait for you. She must have come in through the little windows or something."

I made a noncommittal sound in response and told her to let me in the house, which I was standing in front of. It would be better to not wake her parents with the doorbell. Ellie hung up immediately and not two seconds later had the front door wide open.

She was wearing bright yellow pajama pants, unlike any of the dark clothes I normally saw her in, with hair flattened completely against one side of her head. Without speaking she grabbed my hand and dragged me inside toward the basement and gestured at it angrily, glaring at me as if the whole thing was my fault. Thinking back, it might have been. I unlocked the door and walked halfway down the carpeted stairs.

"Ashlinn?" I called out hopefully into the darkness.

"Victoria!"

It had been far too long since I last heard that voice in person.

She rushed over to the bottom of the stairs, and before I could even make my way down toward her outline, she raced up to me. A pair of awkwardly fitting gym shorts had been added to the sweater Ellie had already told me she was wearing, but there was no time to process her attire. Ashlinn plowed into me, making us both fall back onto the staircase and skid down a step or two.

"Oh my God," I gasped, running my fingers over her hair, "you really are here. This is real. You are my girlfriend and you're here and now I can tell everyone."

It was time to get it out. I took a deep breath and looked her dead in the eyes. "I love you, Ashlinn."

She flashed me her white teeth, unsurprised, and I felt weightless instead of empty. "Indeed. And now we can do this as much as we want," she said, nuzzling into me. The stairs were starting to dig into my contorted back and rug burn was inevitable, but that was easily ignored until a throat was cleared above us.

"I brought you here to get her out of my house, and now you're cuddling on the stairs. Have I missed something?"

Ellie seemed unmoved by whatever grandiose declarations had just occurred and was standing livid in the doorway, which I could see upside down when I tilted my head back. Ashlinn began climbing off me gracelessly in the small space.

"Sorry I scared you so much. Let me try to explain."

Ellie nodded, her expression carved out of marble. "Okay, but not in this house. We're going for a walk."

We clambered up the stairs as Ellie left a note for her parents much like the one I'd left for mine and led us out the door. Before we even got off her property or could begin discussing the incident, Ellie asked me how I was doing. It was sweet that after the morning she had, she was still worried about how I was coping with Reeves's passing. Maybe that would excuse one of her previous dick moves. I tried to put into words how surprisingly okay I was, and she accepted my answer with a grain of salt.

The sidewalk offered us miles of discussion space, and the three of us must have looked like quite a group. All in pajamas and some without shoes. Ellie began her well-deserved cross-examination, and I braced myself. Lying wasn't my forte, nor Ashlinn's or Ellie's either.

"Why did you break into my house?"

"I was lost," Ashlinn began, and it was an obviously rehearsed and poorly constructed fib. I wondered how long she had been in that basement. "I wanted to go to Victoria's place but couldn't find my way, and yours seemed like the next best bet."

Even though her words came slowly, I couldn't help but cheer her on in my mind. This was better than anything I could have thought up.

"How the hell do you even know where I live?"

Ashlinn looked even more tripped up but rescued her story by saying, "I saw The Hovercraft in the driveway."

Ellie stopped walking. "So you're trying to tell me you were walking around town naked so early in the morning it's practically night and thought it'd be a good idea to—what? Crawl in through my tiny excuse for a window so you could use me to find your girlfriend? Does no one else realize how insane that is?"

We both stared at Ellie. She had a point.

"I wasn't having a very good night," Ashlinn tried, although the statement came out more like a question.

"Yeah, well neither was she I imagine," Ellie responded, pointing in my direction but still focused on Ashlinn. "You weren't even at the funeral. What kind of girlfriend are you?"

"Please stop." I knew she deserved an answer but this was a bit much. "It's okay, I promise. She wasn't able to come, and I understand."

"Must've been a hell of an excuse," Ellie grumbled and began walking twice as fast. I ran to catch up.

"It really was."

Stopping yet again, Ellie looked me straight on for a few moments, assessing whatever she saw there. "This has something to do with you asking me all those crazy questions about what I believe in, doesn't it? Are you sure you're all right?"

Returning her gaze with unwavering certainty, I said, "Absolutely. You have to trust me because I'm not positive if there's any way I'll ever be able to explain how I came to meet Ashlinn or what she is."

"*What* she is?" Ellie asked, looking over my shoulder at the girl in question.

"It's really, really complicated."

"And I'm not convinced I want to get involved. Look, I'm not even going to pretend like I understand you guys. I don't get this relationship, and I don't know why Ashlinn was naked in my room. Hell, I barely know her, but if she makes you happy, I can't give her all that much crap about it. For the past year, I've really wanted you to be happy. I guess since you've made your choice I'll accept that lame-ass story about The Hovercraft." She directed her stare toward Ashlinn and said, "Just be good to her, okay? Try not to break this one's heart. Lord knows she deserves that much. And please don't break into my house again, or I *will* call the cops. I have mace and will be sleeping with it from now on. Knock on the door next time."

"I'll do my best. Both with the not scaring you and with treating Victoria well."

Ellie accepted this grimly. "I can't ask any more of you. Keep the clothes. I'm going back home. Seems like you two could use some time alone, and I wanna get back before the parentals awaken. And don't even bother asking me to drive you home. I'm still pissed and deserve some payback."

"Wouldn't dream of it," I assured her.

She gave a weak wave and turned her back to us, stuffing her hands into the tiny pajama pockets. The second she walked out of sight, I all but leapt on top of Ashlinn.

"Welcome to reality. Now care to explain what actually happened?"

She laughed and bent backward to try and balance us so that we wouldn't fall into the road.

"It appears you didn't sleep last night so I wasn't able to sneak into your head and use your dreams to get out. Ellie's fantasies were floating by, and I figured that was the next best thing. Not really my most intelligent decision, but impulses happen and I wanted to see you. Do you know how excited I am to actually have a life now?"

"Hopefully as excited as I am to share it with you."

"And it'll be a great one too," she said with an uncontrollable smile. "I may have acted on that promise to visit those admissions officers."

"You are an absolute dream."

Chisel this moment out of diamonds.

"Not anymore, but I'm ready to have a few of my own. Care to lead the way?"

"I'd love nothing more. I already have an idea of where to head."

Ashlinn laced her fingers in mine as I led us across the empty street in the direction of the rising sun. "Oh, and which way it that?"

"Toward a supermarket. My intention was to take you to an ice cream shop when you first arrived, but they won't be open this early. Instead we're going to act like hungover average teenagers and buy a mountain of Ben and Jerry's, or at least as much as we can get with the money left, and we'll eat it on the curb and count the colors of cars. Later I'll introduce you to Mother, or I can give you a bath, and we can cuddle and talk about how we'll make this all work out, and everything will be perfect."

She stared up at the cotton-candy sky. "It already is."

CALISTA LYNNE is a perpetual runaway who grew up on the American East Coast and is currently studying theater in London. She is oftentimes seen screeching at Big Ben and pointing out the same landmarks on a daily basis, and is having difficulty adjusting to the lack of Oxford commas across the pond. She writes because it always seemed to make more sense than mathematics, and has superb parents who support more than just her latte addiction. If Calista Lynne could change one thing about her life, it'd probably be her lack of ability to play both of the ukuleles adorning her rainbow bookshelves.

Tumblr: calista-lynne.tumblr.com
E-mail: officialcalista@gmail.com
Twitter: @calistawrites

Also from Harmony Ink Press

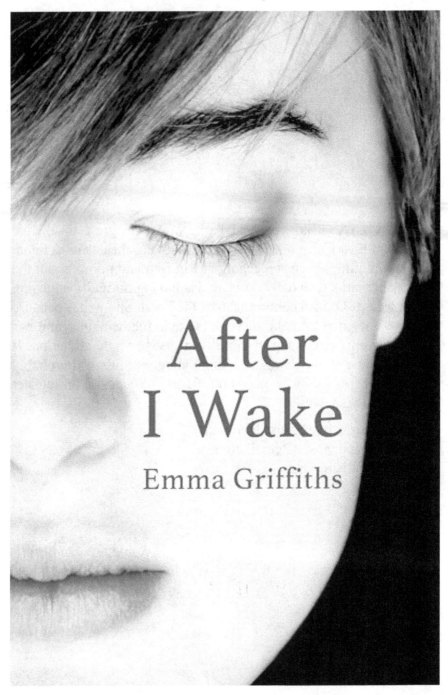

After
I Wake

Emma Griffiths

www.harmonyinkpress.com

Also from Harmony Ink Press

www.harmonyinkpress.com

FOR MORE
OF THE BEST
TEEN & NEW
ADULT FICTION

Harmony Ink

VISIT

HARMONYINKPRESS.COM